Thomas Nelson Page

Elsket, and other stories

Thomas Nelson Page

Elsket, and other stories

ISBN/EAN: 9783743367524

Manufactured in Europe, USA, Canada, Australia, Japa

Cover: Foto ©Andreas Hilbeck / pixelio.de

Manufactured and distributed by brebook publishing software (www.brebook.com)

Thomas Nelson Page

Elsket, and other stories

ELSKET, AND OTHER STORIES

ELSKET

AND OTHER STORIES

BY

THOMAS NELSON PAGE

NEW YORK
CHARLES SCRIBNER'S SONS
1893

TO HER MEMORY

CONTENTS.

vii

ELSKET.

"The knife hangs loose in the sheath."
— OLD NORSK PROVERB.

I SPENT a month of the summer of 188– in Norway — "Old Norway" — and a friend of mine, Dr. John Robson, who is as great a fisherman as he is a physician, and knows that I love a stream where the trout and I can meet each other alone, and have it out face to face, uninterrupted by any interlopers, did me a favor to which I was indebted for the experience related below. He had been to Norway two years before, and he let me into the secret of an unexplored region between the Nord Fiord and the Romsdal. I cannot give the name of the place, because even now it has not been fully explored, and he bound me by a solemn promise that I would not divulge it to a single soul, actually going to the length of insisting on my adding a formal oath to my affirmation. This I con-

1

sented to because I knew that my friend was
a humorous man, and also because otherwise
he positively refused to inform me where
the streams were about which he had been
telling such fabulous fish stories. "No," he
said, "some of those —— cattle who think
they own the earth and have a right to fool
women at will and know how to fish, will be
poking in there, worrying Olaf and Elsket,
and ruining the fishing, and I'll be —— if I
tell you unless you make oath." My friend
is a swearing man, though he says he swears
for emphasis, not blasphemy, and on this
occasion he swore with extreme solemnity.
I saw that he was in earnest, so made affi-
davit and was rewarded.

"Now," he said, after inquiring about my
climbing capacity in a way which piqued me,
and giving me the routes with a particularity
which somewhat mystified me, "Now I will
write a letter to Olaf of the Mountain and
to Elsket. I once was enabled to do them a
slight service, and they will receive you. It
will take him two or three weeks to get it,
so you may have to wait a little. You must
wait at L—— until Olaf comes down to take
you over the mountain. You may be there

when he gets the letter, or you may have to wait for a couple of weeks, as he does not come over the mountain often. However, you can amuse yourself around L——; only you must always be on hand every night in case Olaf comes."

Although this appeared natural enough to the doctor, it sounded rather curious to me, and it seemed yet more so when he added, " By the way, one piece of advice: don't talk about England to Elsket, and don't ask any questions."

" Who is Elsket? " I asked.

" A daughter of the Vikings, poor thing," he said.

My curiosity was aroused, but I could get nothing further out of him, and set it down to his unreasonable dislike of travelling Englishmen, against whom, for some reason, he had a violent antipathy, declaring that they did not know how to treat women nor how to fish. My friend has a custom of speaking very strongly, and I used to wonder at the violence of his language, which contrasted strangely with his character; for he was the kindest-hearted man I ever knew, being a true follower of his patron saint, old Isaac giving his sympathy to all the unfortunate, and even handling his frogs as if he loved them.

Thus it was that on the afternoon of the seventh day of July, 188–, having, for purposes of identification, a letter in my pocket to "Olaf of the Mountain from his friend Dr. Robson," I stood, in the rain in the so-called "street" of L——, on the —— Fiord, looking over the bronzed faces of the stolid but kindly peasants who lounged silently around, trying to see if I could detect in one a resemblance to the picture I had formed in my mind of "Olaf of the Mountain," or could discern in any eye a gleam of special interest to show that its possessor was on the watch for an expected guest.

There was none in whom I could discover any indication that he was not a resident of the straggling little settlement. They all stood quietly about gazing at me and talking in low tones among themselves, chewing tobacco or smoking their pipes, as naturally as if they were in Virginia or Kentucky, only, if possible, in a somewhat more ruminant manner. It gave me the single bit of home feeling I could muster, for it was, I must confess, rather desolate standing alone in a strange land, under those beetling crags, with the clouds almost resting on our heads, and the rain coming down in a steady, wet, monotonous fashion. The half-dozen little dark log or frame-houses, with their double windows and turf roofs, standing about at all sorts of angles to the road, as if they had rolled down the mountain like the great bowlders beyond them, looked dark and cheerless. I was weak enough to wish for a second that I had waited a few days for the rainy spell to be over, but two little bare-headed children, coming down the road laughing and chattering, recalled me to myself. They had no wrapping whatever, and nothing on their heads but their soft flaxen hair, yet they minded the rain no more than if they had been ducklings. I saw that these people were used to rain. It was the inheritance of a thousand years. Something, however, had to be done, and I recognized the fact that I was out of the beaten track of tourists, and that if I had to stay here a week, on the prudence of my first step depended the consideration I should receive. It would not do to be hasty. I had a friend with me

which had stood me in good stead before,
and I applied to it now. Walking slowly
up to the largest, and one of the oldest men
in the group, I drew out my pipe and a bag
of old Virginia tobacco, free from any flavor
than its own, and filling the pipe, I asked
him for a light in the best phrase-book Norsk
I could command. He gave it, and I placed
the bag in his hand and motioned him to
fill his pipe. When that was done I handed
the pouch to another, and motioned him to
fill and pass the tobacco around. One by one
they took it, and I saw that I had friends.
No man can fill his pipe from another's bag
and not wish him well.

"Does any of you know Olaf of the Mountain?" I asked. I saw at once that I had
made an impression. The mention of that
name was evidently a claim to consideration.
There was a general murmur of surprise,
and the group gathered around me. A half-
dozen spoke at once.

"He was at L—— last week," they said, as
if that fact was an item of extensive interest.

"I want to go there," I said, and then
was, somehow, immediately conscious that
I had made a mistake. Looks were ex-

changed and some words were spoken among my friends, as if they were oblivious of my presence.

"You cannot go there. None goes there but at night," said one, suggestively.

"Who goes over the mountain comes no more," said another, as if he quoted a proverb, at which there was a faint intimation of laughter on the part of several.

My first adviser undertook a long explanation, but though he labored faithfully I could make out no more than that it was something about "Elsket" and "the Devil's Ledge," and men who had disappeared. This was a new revelation. What object had my friend? He had never said a word of this. Indeed, he had, I now remembered, said very little at all about the people. He had exhausted his eloquence on the fish. I recalled his words when I asked him about Elsket: "She is a daughter of the Vikings, poor thing." That was all. Had he been up to a practical joke? If so, it seemed rather a sorry one to me just then. But anyhow I could not draw back now. I could never face him again if I did not go on, and what was more serious, I could never face myself.

I was weak enough to have a thought that, after all, the mysterious Olaf might not come; but the recollection of the fish of which my friend had spoken as if they had been the golden fish of the " Arabian Nights," banished that. I asked about the streams around L——. " Yes, there was good fishing." But they were all too anxious to tell me about the danger of going over the mountain to give much thought to the fishing. "No one without Olaf's blood could cross the Devil's Ledge." " Two men had disappeared three years ago." " A man had disappeared there last year. He had gone, and had never been heard of afterward. The Devil's Ledge was a bad pass."

" Why don't they look into the matter? " I asked.

The reply was as near a shrug of the shoulders as a Norseman can accomplish.

"It was not easy to get the proof; the mountain was very dangerous, the glacier very slippery; there were no witnesses," etc. "Olaf of the Mountain was not a man to trouble."

" He hates Englishmen," said one, significantly.

"I am not an Englishman, I am an American," I explained.

This had a sensible effect. Several began to talk at once. One had a brother in Idaho, another had cousins in Nebraska, and so on.

The group had by this time been augmented by the addition of almost the entire population of the settlement; one or two rosy-cheeked women, having babies in their arms, standing in the rain utterly regardless of the steady downpour.

It was a propitious time. " Can I get a place to stay here? " I inquired of the group generally.

" Yes, — oh, yes." There was a consultation in which the name of " Hendrik " was heard frequently, and then a man stepped forward and taking up my bag and rod-case, walked off, I following, escorted by a number of my new friends.

I had been installed in Hendrik's little house about an hour, and we had just finished supper, when there was a murmur outside, and then the door opened, and a young man stepping in, said something so rapidly that I understood only that it concerned Olaf of the Mountain, and in some way myself.

"Olaf of the Mountain is here and wants to speak to you," said my host. "Will you go?"

"Yes," I said. "Why does he not come in?"

"He will not come in," said my host; "he never does come in."

"He is at the church-yard," said the messenger; "he always stops there." They both spoke broken English.

I arose and went out, taking the direction indicated. A number of my friends stood in the road or street as I passed along, and touched their caps to me, looking very queer in the dim twilight. They gazed at me curiously as I walked by.

I turned the corner of a house which stood half in the road, and just in front of me, in its little yard, was the little white church with its square, heavy, short spire. At the gate stood a tall figure, perfectly motionless, leaning on a long staff. As I approached I saw that he was an elderly man. He wore a long beard, once yellow but now gray, and he looked very straight and large. There was something grand about him as he stood there in the dusk.

I came quite up to him. He did not move.

" Good-evening," I said.

" Good-evening."

" Are you Mr. Hovedsen? " I asked, drawing out my letter.

" I am Olaf of the Mountain," he said slowly, as if his name embraced the whole title.

I handed him the letter.

" You are —— ? "

" I am —— " taking my cue from his own manner.

" The friend of her friend? "

" His great friend."

" Can you climb? "

" I can."

" Are you steady ? "

" Yes."

" It is well ; are you ready? "

I had not counted on this, and involuntarily I asked, in some surprise, " To-night? "

" To-night. You cannot go in the day."

I thought of the speech I had heard: " No one goes over the mountain except at night," and the ominous conclusion, " Who goes over the mountain comes no more." My strange host, however, diverted my thoughts.

" A stranger cannot go except at night,"

he said, gravely; and then added, "I must get back to watch over Elsket."

"I shall be ready in a minute," I said, turning.

In ten minutes I had bade good-by to my simple hosts, and leaving them with a sufficient evidence of my consideration to secure their lasting good-will, I was on my way down the street again with my light luggage on my back. This time the entire population of the little village was in the road, and as I passed along I knew by their murmuring conversation that they regarded my action with profound misgiving. I felt, as I returned their touch of the cap and bade them good-by, a little like the gladiators of old who, about to die, saluted Cæsar.

At the gate my strange guide, who had not moved from the spot where I first found him, insisted on taking my luggage, and buckling his straps around it and flinging it over his back, he handed me his stick, and without a word strode off straight toward the black mountain whose vast wall towered above us to the clouds.

I shall never forget that climb.

We were hardly out of the road before we

began to ascend, and I had shortly to stop
for breath. My guide, however, if silent was
thoughtful, and he soon caught my gait and
knew when to pause. Up through the dusk we
went, he guiding me now by a word telling
me how to step, or now turning to give me his
hand to help me up a steep place, over a large
rock, or around a bad angle. For a time we
had heard the roar of the torrent as it boiled
below us, but as we ascended it had gradually
hushed, and we at length were in a region of
profound silence. The night was cloudy, and
as dark as it ever is in midsummer in that
far northern latitude; but I knew that we
were climbing along the edge of a precipice,
on a narrow ledge of rock along the face
of the cliff. The vast black wall above us
rose sheer up, and I could feel rather than
see that it went as sheer down, though my
sight could not penetrate the darkness which
filled the deep abyss below. We had been
climbing about three hours when suddenly
the ledge seemed to die out. My guide
stopped, and unwinding his rope from his
waist, held it out to me. I obeyed his silent
gesture, and binding it around my body gave
him the end. He wrapped it about him,

and then taking me by the arm, as if I had been a child, he led me slowly along the narrow ledge around the face of the wall, step by step, telling me where to place my feet, and waiting till they were firmly planted. I began now to understand why no one ever went "over the mountain" in the day. We were on a ledge nearly three thousand feet high. If it had not been for the strong, firm hold on my arm, I could not have stood it. As it was I dared not think. Suddenly we turned a sharp angle and found ourselves in a curious semicircular place, almost level and fifty or sixty feet deep in the concave, as if a great piece had been gouged out of the mountain by the glacier which must once have been there.

"This is a curious place," I ventured to say.

"It is," said my guide. "It is the Devil's Seat. Men have died here."

His tone was almost fierce. I accepted his explanation silently. We passed the singular spot and once more were on the ledge, but except in one place it was not so narrow as it had been the other side of the Devil's Seat, and in fifteen minutes we had crossed the summit and the path widened a little and began to descend.

"You do well," said my guide, briefly, " but not so well as Doctor John." I was well content with being ranked a good second to the doctor just then.

The rain had ceased, the sky had partly cleared, and, as we began to descend, the early twilight of the northern dawn began to appear. First the sky became a clear steel-gray and the tops of the mountains became visible, the dark outlines beginning to be filled in, and taking on a soft color. This lightened rapidly, until on the side facing east they were bathed in an atmosphere so clear and transparent that they seemed almost within a stone's throw of us, while the other side was still left in a shadow which was so deep as to be almost darkness. The gray lightened and lightened into pearl until a tinge of rose appeared, and then the sky suddenly changed to the softest blue, and a little later the snow-white mountain-tops were bathed in pink, and it was day.

I could see in the light that we were descending into a sort of upland hollow between the snow-patched mountain-tops; below us

was a lovely little valley in which small pines
and birches grew, and patches of the green,
short grass which stands for hay shone among
the great bowlders.   Several little streams
came jumping down as white as milk from
the glaciers stuck between the mountain-tops,
and after resting in two or three tiny lakes
which looked like hand-mirrors lying in the
grass below, went bubbling and foaming on
to the edge of the precipice, over which they
sprang, to be dashed into vapor and snow
hundreds of feet down.   A half-dozen sheep
and as many goats were feeding about in the
little valley; but I could not see the least
sign of a house, except a queer, brown struct-
ure, on a little knoll, with many gables and
peaks, ending in the curious dragon-pennants,
which I recognized as one of the old Norsk
wooden churches of a past age.

When, however, an hour later, we had got
down to the table-land, I found myself suddenly in front of a long, quaint, double log
cottage, set between two immense bowlders,
and roofed with layers of birch bark, covered
with turf, which was blue with wild pansies.
It was as if it were built under a bed of
heart's-ease.   It was very old, and had evi-

dently been a house of some pretension, for there was much curious carving about the doors, and indeed about the whole front, the dragon's head being distinctly visible in the design. There were several lesser houses which looked as if they had once been dwellings, but they seemed now to be only stables.

As we approached the principal door it was opened, and there stepped forth one of the most striking figures I ever saw — a young woman, rather tall, and as straight as an arrow. My friend's words involuntarily recurred to me, "A daughter of the Vikings," and then, somehow, I too had the feeling he had expressed, "Poor thing!" Her figure was one of the richest and most perfect I ever beheld. Her face was singularly beautiful; but it was less her beauty than her nobility of look and mien combined with a certain sadness which impressed me. The features were clear and strong and perfectly carved. There was a firm mouth, a good jaw, strong chin, a broad brow, and deep blue eyes which looked straight at you. Her expression was so soft and tender as to have something pathetic in it. Her hair was flaxen, and as fine as satin, and was brushed perfectly smooth

and coiled on the back of her shapely head,
which was placed admirably on her shoulders.
She was dressed in the coarse, black-blue
stuff of the country, and a kerchief, also dark
blue, was knotted under her chin, and fell
back behind her head, forming a dark background for her silken hair.

Seeing us she stood perfectly still until we
drew near, when she made a quaint, low
courtesy and advanced to meet her father
with a look of eager expectancy in her large
eyes.

" Elsket," he said, with a tenderness which
conveyed the full meaning of the sweet pet
term, " darling."

There was something about these people,
peasants though they were, which gave me
a strange feeling of respect for them.

" This is Doctor John's friend," said the
old man, quietly.

She looked at her father in a puzzled way
for a moment, as if she had not heard him,
but as he repeated his introduction a light
came into her eyes, and coming up to me she
held out her hand, saying, " Welcome."

Then turning to her father — "Have you
a letter for me, father ?" she asked.

"No, Elsket," he said, gently; "but I will go again next month."

A cloud settled on her face and increased its sadness, and she turned her head away. After a moment she went into the house and I saw that she was weeping. A look of deep dejection came over the old man's face also.

II.

I found that my friend, "Doctor John," strange to relate of a fisherman, had not exaggerated the merits of the fishing. How they got there, two thousand feet above the lower valley, I don't know; but trout fairly swarmed in the little streams, which boiled among the rocks, and they were as greedy as if they had never seen a fly in their lives. I shortly became contemptuous toward anything under three pounds, and addressed myself to the task of defending my flies against the smaller ones, and keeping them only for the big fellows, which ran over three pounds — the patriarchs of the streams. With these I had capital sport, for they knew every angle and hole, they sought every coign

of vantage, and the rocks were so thick and
so sharp that from the time one of these vet-
erans took the fly, it was an equal contest
which of us should come off victorious. I
was often forced to rush splashing and floun-
dering through the water to my waist to keep
my line from being sawed, and as the water
was not an hour from the green glaciers
above, it was not always entirely pleasant.

I soon made firm friends with my hosts,
and varied the monotony of catching three-
pounders by helping them get in their hay
for the winter. Elsket, poor thing, was,
notwithstanding her apparently splendid
physique, so delicate that she could no longer
stand the fatigue of manual labor, any extra
exertion being liable to bring on a recurrence
of the heart-failure, from which she had suf-
fered. I learned that she had had a violent
hemorrhage two summers before, from which
she had come near dying, and that the skill
of my friend, the doctor, had doubtless saved
her life. This was the hold he had on Olaf
of the Mountain: this was the "small service"
he had rendered them.

By aiding them thus, I was enabled to be
of material assistance to Olaf, and I found in

helping these good people, that work took on once more the delight which I remembered it used to have under like circumstances when I was a boy. I could cut or carry on my back loads of hay all day, and feel at night as if I had been playing. Such is the singular effect of the spirit on labor.

To make up for this, Elsket would sometimes, when I went fishing, take her knitting and keep me company, sitting at a little distance. With her pale, calm face and shining hair outlined against the background of her sad-colored kerchief, she looked like a mourning angel. I never saw her smile except when her father came into her presence, and when she smiled it was as if the sun had suddenly come out. I began to understand the devotion of these two strange people, so like and yet so different.

One rainy day she had a strange turn; she began to be restless. Her large, sad eyes, usually so calm, became bright; the two spots in her cheeks burned yet deeper; her face grew anxious. Then she laid her knitting aside and took out of a great chest something on which she began to sew busily. I was looking at her, when she caught my eye

and smiled. It was the first time she ever
smiled for me. "Did you know I was going
to be married?" she asked, just as an American girl might have done. And before I
could answer, she brought me the work. It
was her wedding dress. "I have nearly
finished it," she said. Then she brought me
a box of old silver ornaments, such as the
Norsk brides wear, and put them on. When
I had admired them she put them away.
After a little, she arose and began to wander
about the house and out into the rain. I
watched her with interest. Her father came
in, and I saw a distressed look come into his
eyes. He went up to her, and laying his
hand on her drew her toward a seat. Then
taking down an old Bible, he turned to a
certain place and began to read. He read
first the Psalm: "Lord, thou hast been our
refuge, from one generation to another. Before the mountains were brought forth, or
ever the earth and the world were made, thou
art God from everlasting, and world without
end." Then he turned to the chapter of
Corinthians, "Now is Christ risen from the
dead, and become the first-fruits of them that
slept," etc. His voice was clear, rich, and

devout, and he read it with singular earnestness and beauty. It gave me a strange feeling; it is a part of our burial service. Then he opened his hymn-book and began to sing a low, dirge-like hymn. I sat silent, watching the strange service and noting its effect on Elsket. She sat at first like a person bound, struggling to be free, then became quieter, and at last, perfectly calm. Then Olaf knelt down, and with his hand still on her prayed one of the most touching prayers I ever heard. It was for patience.

When he rose Elsket was weeping, and she went and leant in his arms like a child, and he kissed her as tenderly as if he had been her mother.

Next day, however, the same excited state recurred, and this time the reading appeared to have less effect. She sewed busily, and insisted that there must be a letter for her at L——. A violent fit of weeping was followed by a paroxysm of coughing, and finally the old man, who had sat quietly by her with his hand stroking her head, arose and said, "I will go." She threw herself into his arms, rubbing her head against him in sign of dumb affection, and in a little while grew calm. It was still raining and quite late, only a little before sunset; but the old man went out, and taking the path toward L——— was soon climbing the mountain toward the Devil's Seat. Elsket sat up all night, but she was as calm and as gentle as ever.

The next morning when Olaf returned she went out to meet him. Her look was full of eager expectancy. I did not go out, but watched her from the door. I saw Olaf shake his head, and heard her say bitterly, "It is so hard to wait," and he said, gently, "Yes, it is, Elsket, but I will go again," and then she came in weeping quietly, the old man following with a tender look on his strong, weather-beaten face.

That day Elsket was taken ill. She had been trying to do a little work in the field in the afternoon, when a sinking spell had come on. It looked for a time as if the poor over-driven heart had knocked off work for good and all. Strong remedies, however, left by Doctor John, set it going again, and we got her to bed. She was still desperately feeble, and Olaf sat up. I could not leave him, so we were sitting watching, he one side the open platform fireplace in one corner, and I the other; he smoking, anxious, silent, grim; I watching the expression on his gray face. His eyes seemed set back deeper than ever under the shaggy gray brows, and as the firelight fell on him he had the fierce, hopeless look of a caged eagle. It was late in the night before he spoke, and then it was half to himself and but half to me.

"I have fought it ten long years," he said, slowly.

Not willing to break the thread of his thought by speaking, I lit my pipe afresh and just looked at him. He received it as an answer.

"She is the last of them," he said, accepting me as an auditor rather than addressing me. "We go back to Olaf Traetelje, the blood of Harold Haarfager (the Fairhaired) is in our veins, and here it ends. Dane and Swede have known our power, Saxon and Celt have bowed bare-headed to us, and with her it ends. In this stronghold many times her fathers have found refuge from their foes and gained breathing-time after battles by sea and land. From this nest, like eagles, they have swooped down, carrying all before them, and here, at last, when betrayed and

hunted, they found refuge. Here no foreign
king could rule over them; here they learnt
the lesson that Christ is the only king, and
that all men are his brothers. Here they
lived and worshipped him. If their domin-
ions were stolen from them they found here a
truer wealth, content; if they had not power,
they had what was better, independence. For
centuries they held this last remnant of the
dominion which Harold Haarfager had con-
quered by land, and Eric of the Bloody Axe
had won by sea, sending out their sons and
daughters to people the lands; but the race
dwindled as their lands had done before, and
now with her dies the last. How has it
come? As ever, by betrayal!"

The old man turned fiercely, his breast
heaving, his eyes burning.

"Was she who came of a race at whose
feet jarls have crawled and kings have knelt
not good enough?" I was hearing the story
and did not interrupt him — "Not good
enough for him!" he continued in his low,
fierce monotone. "I did not want him. What
if he was a Saxon? His fathers were our boat-
men. Rather Cnut a thousand times. Then
the race would not have died. Then she
would not be — not be so."

The reference to her recalled him to himself, and he suddenly relapsed into silence.

" At least, Cnut paid the score," he began once more, in a low intense undertone. " In his arms he bore him down from the Devil's Seat, a thousand feet sheer on the hard ice, where his cursed body lies crushed forever, a witness of his falsehood."

I did not interrupt, and he rewarded my patience, giving a more connected account, for the first time addressing me directly.

" Her mother died when she was a child," he said, softly. His gentle voice contrasted strangely with the fierce undertone in which he had been speaking. " I was mother as well as father to her. She was as good as she was beautiful, and each day she grew more and more so. She was a second Igenborg. Knowing that she needed other companionship than an old man, I sought and brought her Cnut (he spoke of him as if I must know all about him). Cnut was the son of my only kinsman, the last of his line as well, and he was tall and straight and strong. I loved him and he was my son, and as he grew I saw that he loved her, and I was not sorry, for he was goodly to look on, straight and tall as one of

old, and he was good also. And she was satisfied with him, and from a child ordered him
to do her girlish bidding, and he obeyed and
laughed, well content to have her smile. And
he would carry her on his shoulder, and take
her on the mountain to slide, and would gather
her flowers. And I thought it was well. And
I thought that in time they would marry and
have the farm, and that there would be
children about the house, and the valley
might be filled with their voices as in the
old time. And I was content. And one
day *he* came! (the reference cost him an
effort). Cnut found him fainting on the
mountain and brought him here in his arms.
He had come to the village alone, and the idle
fools there had told him of me, and he had
asked to meet me, and they told him of the
mountain, and that none could pass the Devil's
Ledge but those who had the old blood, and
that I loved not strangers; and he said he
would pass it, and he had come and passed
safely the narrow ledge, and reached the
Devil's Seat, when a stone had fallen upon
him, and Cnut had found him there fainting, and had lifted him and brought him
here, risking his own life to save him on the

ledge. And he was near to death for days, and she nursed him and brought him from the grave.

"At first I was cold to him, but there was something about him that drew me and held me. It was not that he was young and taller than Cnut, and fair. It was not that his eyes were clear and full of light, and his figure straight as a young pine. It was not that he had climbed the mountain and passed the narrow ledge and the Devil's Seat alone, though I liked well his act; for none but those who have Harold Haarfager's blood have done it alone in all the years, though many have tried and failed. I asked him what men called him, and he said, 'Harold;' then laughing, said some called him, 'Harold the Fair-haired.' The answer pleased me. There was something in the name which drew me to him. When I first saw him I had thought of Harald Haarfager, and of Harald Haardraarder, and of that other Harold, who, though a Saxon, died bravely for his kingdom when his brother betrayed him, and I held out my hand and gave him the clasp of friendship."

The old man paused, but after a brief reflection proceeded:

" We made him welcome and we loved him. He knew the world and could tell us many things. He knew the story of Norway and the Vikings, and the Sagas were on his tongue. Cnut loved him and followed him, and she (the pause which always indicated her who filled his thoughts) — she, then but a girl, laughed and sang for him, and he sang for her, and his voice was rich and sweet. And she went with him to fish and to climb, and often, when Cnut and I were in the field, we would hear her laugh, clear and fresh from the rocks beside the streams, as he told her some fine story of his England. He stayed here a month and a week, and then departed, saying he would come again next year, and the house was empty and silent after he left. But after a time we grew used to it once more and the winter came.

" When the spring returned we got a letter —a letter to her—saying he would come again, and every two weeks another letter came, and I went for it and brought it to — to her, and she read it to Cnut and me. And at last he came and I went to meet him, and brought him here, welcome as if he had been my eldest born, and we were glad. Cnut smiled and

ran forward and gave him his hand, and—
she—she did not come at first, but when she
came she was clad in all that was her best,
and wore her silver—the things her mother
and her grandmother had worn, and as she
stepped out of the door and saluted him, I
saw for the first time that she was a woman
grown, and it was hard to tell which face was
brighter, hers or his, and Cnut smiled to see
her so glad."

The old man relapsed into reflection.
Presently, however, he resumed:

" This time he was gayer than before:—the
summer seemed to come with him. He sang
to her and read to her from books that he
had brought, teaching her to speak English
like himself, and he would go and fish up the
streams while she sat near by and talked to
him. Cnut also learned his tongue well, and
I did also, but Cnut did not see so much of
him as before, for Cnut had to work, and in
the evening they were reading and she—she
—grew more and more beautiful, and laughed
and sang more. And so the summer passed.
The autumn came, but he did not go, and I
was well content, for she was happy, and, in
truth, the place was cheerier that he was here.

Cnut alone seemed downcast, but I knew not why; and then the snow came. One morning we awoke and the farm was as white as the mountains. I said to him, 'Now you are here for the winter,' and he laughed and said, 'No, I will stay till the new-year. I have business then in England, and I must go.' And I turned, and her face was like sunshine, for she knew that none but Cnut and I had ever passed the Devil's Ledge in the snow, and the other way by which I took the Doctor home was worse then, though easier in the summer, only longer. But Cnut looked gloomy, at which I chid him; but he was silent. And the autumn passed rapidly, so cheerful was he, finding in the snow as much pleasure as in the sunshine, and taking her out to slide and race on shoes till she would come in with her cheeks like roses in summer, and her eyes like stars, and she made it warm where she was.

"And one evening they came home. He was gayer than ever, and she more beautiful, but silenter than her wont. She looked like her mother the evening I asked her to be my wife. I could not take my eyes from her. That night Cnut was a caged wolf. At last he asked me to come out, and then he told me that he had seen Harold kiss her and had heard him tell her that he loved her, and she had not driven him away. My heart was wrung for Cnut, for I loved him, and he wept like a child. I tried to comfort him, but it was useless, and the next day he went away for a time. I was glad to have him go, for I grieved for him, and I thought she would miss him and be glad when he came again, and though the snow was bad on the mountain he was sure as a wolf. He bade us goodby and left with his eyes looking like a hurt dog's. I thought she would have wept to have him go, but she did not. She gave him her hand and turned back to Harold, and smiled to him when he smiled. It was the first time in all her life that I had not been glad to have her smile, and I was sorry Harold had stayed, and I watched Cnut climb the mountain like a dark speck against the snow till he disappeared. She was so happy and beautiful that I could not long be out with her, though I grieved for Cnut, and when she came to me and told me one night of her great love for Harold I forgot my own regret in her joy, and I said nothing to Harold, because she told me he said that in his country it was not usual for the father to be told or to speak to a daughter's lover.

"They were much taken up together after that, and I was alone, and I missed Cnut sorely, and would have longed for him more but for her happiness. But one day, when he had been gone two months, I looked over the mountain, and on the snow I saw a black speck. It had not been there before, and I watched it as it moved, and I knew it was Cnut.

"I said nothing until he came, and then I ran and met him. He was thin, and worn, and older; but his eyes had a look in them which I thought was joy at getting home; only they were not soft, and he looked taller than when he left, and he spoke little. His eyes softened when she, hearing his voice, came out and held out her hand to him, smiling to welcome him; but he did not kiss her as kinsfolk do after long absence, and when Harold came out the wolf-look came back into his eyes. Harold looked not so pleased to see him, but held out his hand to greet him. But Cnut stepped back, and suddenly drawing from his breast a letter placed it in his palm, saying slowly, ' I have been to England, Lord Harold, and have brought you this from your Lady Ethelfrid Penrith — they expect you to your wedding at the New Year.' Harold turned as white as the snow under his feet, and she gave a cry and fell full length on the ground.

" Cnut was the first to reach her, and lifting her in his arms he bore her into the house. Harold would have seized her, but Cnut brushed him aside as if he had been a barley-straw, and carried her and laid her down. When she came to herself she did not remember clearly what had happened. She was strange to me who was her father, but she knew him. I could have slain him, but she called him. He went to her, and she understood only that he was going away, and she wept. He told her it was true that he had loved another woman and had promised to marry her, before he had met her, but now he loved her better, and he would go home and arrange everything and return; and she listened and clung to him. I hated him and wanted him to go, but he was my guest, and I told him that he could not go through the snow; but he was determined. It seemed as if he wanted now to get away, and I was glad to have him go, for my child was strange to me, and if he had deceived one woman I knew he might another, and Cnut said that the letter he had sent by him before the snow came was to say he would come in time to be married at the New Year; and Cnut said he lived in a great castle and owned broad lands, more than one could see from the whole mountain, and his people had brought him in and asked him many questions of him, and had offered him gold to bring the letter back, and he had refused the gold, and brought it without the gold; and some said he had deceived more than one woman. And Lord Harold went to get ready, and she wept, and moaned, and was strange. And then Cnut went to her and told her of his own love for her, and that he was loyal to her, but she waved him from her, and when he asked her to marry him, for he loved her truly, she said him nay with violence, so that he came forth into the air looking white as a leper. And he sat down, and when I came out he was sitting on a stone, and had his knife in his hand, looking at it with a dangerous gleam in his eyes; and just then she arose and came out, and, seeing him sitting so with his knife, she gave a start, and her manner changed, and going to him she spoke softly to him for the first time, and made him yield her up the knife ; for she knew that the knife hung loose in the sheath. But then she changed again and all her anger rose against Cnut, that he had brought Harold the letter which carried him away, and Cnut sat saying nothing, and his face was like stone. Then Lord Harold came and said he was ready, and he asked Cnut would he carry his luggage. And Cnut at first refused, and then suddenly looked him full in his face, and said, ' Yes.' And Harold entered the house to say good-by to her, and I heard her weeping within, and my heart grew hard against the Englishman, and Cnut's face was black with anger, and when Harold came forth I heard her cry out, and he turned in the door and said he would return, and would write her a letter to let her know when he would return. But he said it as one speaks to a child to quiet it, not meaning it. And Cnut went in to speak to her, and I heard her drive him out as if he had been a dog, and he came forth with his face like a wolf's, and taking up Lord Harold's luggage, he set out. And so they went over the mountain.

"And all that night she lay awake, and I heard her moaning, and all next day she sat like stone, and I milked the goats, and her thoughts were on the letters he would send.

"I spoke to her, but she spoke only of the letters to come, and I kept silence, for I had seen that Lord Harold would come no more; for I had seen him burn the little things she had given him, and he had taken everything away, but I could not tell her so. And the days passed, and I hoped that Cnut would come straight back; but he did not. It grieved me, for I loved him, and hoped that he would return, and that in time she would forget Lord Harold, and not be strange, but be as she had been to Cnut before he came. Yet I thought it not wholly wonderful that Cnut did not return at once, nor unwise; for she was lonely, and would sit all day looking up the mountain, and when he came she would, I thought, be glad to have him back.

"At the end of a week she began to urge me to go for a letter. But I told her it could not come so soon; but when another week had passed she began to sew, and when I asked her what she sewed, she said her bridal dress, and she became so that I agreed to go, for I knew no letter would come, and it broke my heart to see her. And when I was ready she kissed me, and wept in my arms, and called me her good father; and so I started.

"She stood in the door and watched me climb the mountain, and waved to me almost gayly.

"The snow was deep, but I followed the track which Cnut and the Englishman had made two weeks before, for no new snow had fallen, and I saw that one track was ever behind the other, and never beside it, as if Cnut had fallen back and followed behind him.

And so I came near to the Devil's Seat, where it was difficult, and from where Cnut had brought him in his arms that day, and then, for the first time, I began to fear, for I remembered Cnut's look as he came from the house when she waved him off, and it had been so easy for him with a swing of his strong arm to have pushed the other over the cliff. But when I saw that he had driven his stick in deep to hold hard, and that the tracks went on beyond, I breathed freely again, and so I passed the narrow path, and the black wall, and came to the Devil's Seat; and as I turned the rock my heart stopped beating, and I had nearly fallen from the ledge. For there, scattered and half-buried in the snow, lay the pack Cnut had carried on his back, and the snow was all dug up and piled about as if stags had been fighting there for their lives. From the wall, across and back, were deep furrows, as if they were ploughed by men's feet dug fiercely in; but they were ever deeper toward the edge, and on one spot at the edge the snow was all torn clear from the black rock, and beyond the seat the narrow path lay smooth, and bright, and level as it had fallen, without a track. My knees shook under me, and I clutched my stick for support, and everything grew black before me: and presently I fell on my knees and crawled and peered over the edge. But there was nothing to be seen, only where the wall slants sharp down for a little space in one spot the snow was brushed away as if something had struck there, and the black, smooth rock showed clean, cutting off the sight from the glacier a thousand feet down."

The old man's breast heaved. It was evidently a painful narrative, but he kept on.

"I sat down in the snow and thought; for I could not think at once. Cnut had not wished to murder, or else he had flung the Englishman from the narrow ledge with one blow of his strong arm. He had waited until they had stood on the Devil's Seat, and then he had thrown off his pack and faced him, man to man. The Englishman was strong and active, taller and heavier than Cnut. He had Harald's name, but he had not Harald's heart nor blood, and Cnut had carried him in his arms over the cliff, with his false heart like water in his body.

"I sat there all day and into the night; for I knew that he would betray no one more. I sorrowed for Cnut, for he was my very son. And after a time I would have gone back to her, but I thought of her at home waiting and watching for me with a letter, and I could not; and then I wept, and I wished that I were Cnut, for I knew that he had had one moment of joy when he took the Englishman in his arms. And then I took the scattered things from the snow and threw them over the cliff; for I would not let it be known that Cnut had flung the Englishman over. It would be talked about over the mountain, and Cnut would be thought a murderer by those who did not know, and some would say he had done it foully; and so I went on over the mountain, and told it there that Cnut and the Englishman had gone over the cliff together in the snow on their way, and it was thought that a slip of snow had carried them. And I came back and told her only that no letter had come."

He was silent so long that I thought he had ended; but presently, in a voice so low that it was just like a whisper, he added: "I thought she would forget, but she has not, and every fortnight she begins to sew her dress and I go over the mountains to give her peace; for each time she draws nearer to the end, and wears away more and more; and some day the thin blade will snap."

"The thin blade" was already snapping, and even while he was speaking the last fibres were giving way.

The silence which followed his words was broken by Elsket; I heard a strange sound, and Elsket called feebly, "Oh, father."

Olaf went quickly to her bedside. I heard him say, "My God in Heaven!" and I sprang up and joined him. It was a hemorrhage.

Her life-blood was flowing from her lips. She could not last like that ten minutes.

Providentially the remedies provided by Doctor John were right at hand, and, thanks to them, the crimson tide was stayed before life went out; but it was soon apparent that her strength was gone and her power exhausted.

We worked over her, but her pulse was running down like a broken clock. There was no time to have got a physician, even had there been one to get. I mentioned it; Olaf shook his head. "She is in the hands of God," he said.

Olaf never left the bedside except to heat water or get some stimulant for her.

But, notwithstanding every effort, she failed to rally. The overtaxed heart was giving out, and all day she sank steadily. I never saw such a desperate face as that old man's. It haunts me now. He hung over her. He held her hand, now growing cold, against his cheek to keep it warm — stroked it and kissed it. As towards evening the short, quick breaths came, which precede dissolution, he sank on his knees. At first, he buried his face in his hands; then in

the agony of his despair, he began to speak
aloud. I never heard a more moving appeal.
It was a man speaking face to face with God
for one about to enter his presence. His eyes
were wide open, as if he saw His face. He
did not ask that she should be spared to him;
it was all for his "Elska," his "Darling,"
that Jesus would be her "Herder," and lead
her beside the still waters; that she might
be spared all suffering and sorrow, and have
peace.

Presently he ended and buried his face in
his hands. The quick, faint breaths had died
away, and as I looked on the still white face
on the pillow I thought that she had gone.
But suddenly the large eyes slowly opened
wide.

"Father," she said, faintly.

"Elsket," the old man bent over her
eagerly.

"I am so tired."

"My Elsket."

"I love you."

"Yes, my Elsket."

"You will stay with me?"

"Yes, always."

"If Cnut comes?"

" Yes, my Elsket."

" If Cnut comes —— " very faintly.

Her true lover's name was the last on her lips.

He bent his ear to her lips. " Yes? "

But we never knew just what she wanted. The dim, large eyes closed, and then the lids lifted slowly a little; there was a sigh, and Elsket's watching was over; the weary spirit was at peace.

" She is with God," he said, calmly.

I closed the white lids gently, and moved out. Later I offered to help him, but he said " No," and I remained out of doors till the afternoon.

About sunset he appeared and went up toward the old church, and I went into the house. I found that he had laid her out in the large room, and she lay with her face slightly turned as if asleep. She was dressed like a bride in the bridal dress she had sewn so long; her hair was unbound, and lay about her, fine and silken, and she wore the old silver ornaments she had showed me. No bride had ever a more faithful attendant. He had put them all upon her.

After a time, as he did not come back, I

went to look for him. As I approached
I heard a dull, thumping sound. When I
reached the cleared place I found him digging. He had chosen a spot just in front of
the quaint old door, with the rude, runic letters, which the earliest sunbeams would touch.
As I came up I saw he was digging her grave.
I offered to help, but he said " No." So I carried him some food and placing it near him
left him.

Late that evening he came down and asked
me if I would sit up that night. I told him,
yes. He thanked me and went into the house.
In a little while he came out and silently went
up the path toward the mountain.

It was a strange night that I spent in that
silent valley in that still house, only I, and
the dead girl lying there so white and peace-
ful. I had strange thoughts, and the earth
and things earthly disappeared for me that
night shut in by those mountain walls. I
was in a world alone. I was cut off from all
but God and the dead. I have dear ones in
heaven, and I was nearer to them that night,
amid the mountain-tops of Norway, than I
was to earthly friends. I think I was nearer
to heaven that night than I ever shall be
again till I get there.

Day broke like a great pearl, but I did not heed it. It was all peace.

Suddenly there was a step outside, and Olaf, with his face drawn and gray, and bowing under the weight of the burden upon his shoulder, stepped wearily in at the door.

To do Elsket honor he had been over the mountain to get it. I helped lift it down and place it, and then he waited for me to go. As I passed out of the door I saw him bend over the quiet sleeper. I looked in later; he had placed her in the coffin, but the top was not on and he was on his knees beside her.

He did not bury her that day; but he never left her side; he sat by her all day and all night. Next day he came to the door and looked at me. I went in and understood that he wanted me to look for the last time on her face. It was fairer than I ever saw it. He had cut her flowers and placed them all about her, and on her breast was a small packet of letters. All care, all suffering, all that was merely of the earth were cleansed away, and she looked as she lay, like a dead angel. After I came out I heard him fastening on the top, and when he finished I went in again. He would have attempted to carry it by him-

self, but I restrained him, and without a word
he took the head and I the foot, and so lifting her tenderly we went gently out and up
toward the church. We had to pause and
rest several times, for he was almost worn out.
After we had lowered her into the grave I
was in doubt what to do; but Olaf drew from
his coat his two books, and standing close by
the side of the grave he opened first the little
Bible and began to read in a low but distinct
voice: "Lord, thou hast been our refuge, from
one generation to another. Before the mountains were brought forth, or ever the earth
and the world were made, thou art God from
everlasting, and world without end."

When he finished this he turned and read
again: "Now is Christ risen from the dead, and
become the first-fruits of them that slept," etc.
They were the Psalm and the chapter which
I had heard him read to Elsket that first day
when she became excited, and with which he
had so often charmed her restless spirit.

He closed, and I thought he was done, but
he opened his hymn-book and turning over a
few leaves sang the same hymn he had sung
to her that day. He sang it all through to
the end, the low, strange, dirge-like hymn,

and chanted as it was by that old man alone,
standing in the fading evening light beside
the grave which he had dug for his daughter,
the last of his race, I never heard anything
so moving. Then he knelt, and clasping his
hands offered a prayer. The words, from
habit, ran almost as they had done when he
had prayed for Elsket before, that God would
be her Shepherd, her "Herder," and lead her
beside the still waters, and give her peace.

When he was through I waited a little, and
then I took up a spade to help him; but he
reached out and took it quietly, and seeing
that he wanted to be alone I left him. He
meant to do for Elsket all the last sacred
offices himself.

I was so fatigued that on reaching the
house I dropped off to sleep and slept till
morning, and I do not know when he came
into the house, if he came at all. When I
waked early next morning he was not there,
and I rose and went up to the church to hunt
for him. He was sitting quietly beside the
grave, and I saw that he had placed at her
head a little cross of birchwood, on which he
had burned one word, simply,

" ELSKET."

I spoke to him, asking him to come to the house.

"I cannot leave her," he said; but when I urged him he rose silently and returned with me.

I remained with him for a while after that, and each day he went and sat by the grave. At last I had to leave. I urged him to come with me, but he replied always, "No, I must watch over Elsket."

It was late in the evening when we set off to cross the mountain. We came by the same path by which I had gone, Olaf leading me as carefully and holding me as steadily as when I went over before. I stopped at the church to lay a few wild flowers on the little gray mound where Elsket slept so quietly. Olaf said not a word; he simply waited till I was done and then followed me dumbly. I was so filled with sorrow for him that I did not, except in one place, think much of the fearful cliffs along which we made our way. At the Devil's Seat, indeed, my nerves for a moment seemed shaken and almost gave way as I thought of the false young lord whose faithlessness had caused all the misery to these simple, kindly folk, and of the fierce young Norseman who had there found so sweet a revenge. But we came on and passed the ledge, and descending struck the broader path just after the day broke, where it was no longer perilous but only painful.

There Olaf paused. " I will go back if you don't want me," he said. I did not need his services, but I urged him to come on with me — to pay a visit to his friends. " I have none," he said, simply. Then to come home with me and live with me in old Virginia. He said, " No," he " must watch over Elsket." So finally I had to give in, and with a clasp of the hand and a message to " her friend " Doctor John, to " remember Elsket," he went back and was soon lost amid the rocks.

I was half-way down when I reached a cleared place an hour or so later, and turned to look back. The sharp angle of the Devil's Ledge was the highest point visible, the very pinnacle of the mountain, and there, clear against the burnished steel of the morning sky, on the very edge, clear in the rare atmosphere was a small figure. It stood for a second, a black point distinctly outlined, and then disappeared.

It was Olaf of the Mountain, gone back to keep watch over Elsket.

"GEORGE WASHINGTON'S" LAST DUEL.

Of all the places in the county "The Towers" was the favorite with the young people. There even before Margaret was installed the Major kept open house with his major domo and factotum "George Washington"; and when Margaret came from school, of course it was popular. Only one class of persons was excluded.

There were few people in the county who did not know of the Major's antipathy to "old women," as he called them. Years no more entered into his definition of this class than celibacy did into his idea of an "old bachelor." The state of single blessedness continued in the female sex beyond the bloom of youth was in his eyes the sole basis of this unpardonable condition. He made certain concessions to the few individuals among his neighbors who had remained in the state of

spinsterhood, because, as he declared, neigh-
borliness was a greater virtue than consistency; but he drew the line at these few, and
it was his boast that no old woman had ever
been able to get into his Eden. "One of
them," he used to say, "would close paradise
just as readily now as Eve did six thousand
years ago." Thus, although as Margaret
grew up she had any other friends she de-
sired to visit her as often as she chose, her
wish being the supreme law at Rock Towers,
she had never even thought of inviting one
of the class against whom her uncle's ruddy
face was so steadfastly set. The first time
it ever occurred to her, to invite any one
among the proscribed was when she asked
Rose Endicott to pay her a visit. Rose, she
knew, was living with her old aunt, Miss
Jemima Bridges, whom she had once met in
R——, and she had some apprehension that
in Miss Jemima's opinion, the condition of
the South was so much like that of the
Sandwich Islands that the old lady would not
permit Rose to come without her personal
escort. Accordingly, one evening after tea,
when the Major was in a particularly gracious
humor, and had told her several of his oldest

and best stories, Margaret fell upon him un-
awares, and before he had recovered from the
shock of the encounter, had captured his con-
sent. Then, in order to secure the leverage
of a dispatched invitation, she had immediately written Rose, asking her and her aunt to
come and spend a month or two with her, and
had without delay handed it to George Washington to deliver to Lazarus to give Luke
to carry to the post-office. The next evening,
therefore, when the Major, after twenty-four
hours of serious apprehension, reopened the
matter with a fixed determination to coax or
buy her out of the notion, because, as he used
to say, "women can't be *reasoned* out of a
thing, sir, not having been reasoned in," Margaret was able to meet him with the announcement that it was "too late," as the letter had
already been mailed.

Seated in one of the high-backed arm-chairs,
with one white hand shading her laughing
eyes from the light, and with her evening
dress daintily spread out about her, Margaret
was amused at the look of desperation on the
old gentleman's ruddy face. He squared his
round body before the fire, braced himself
with his plump legs well apart, as if he were

preparing to sustain the shock of a blow, and taking a deep inspiration, gave a loud and prolonged " Whew ! "

This was too much for her.

Margaret rose, and, going up to him, took his arm and looked into his face cajolingly.

" Uncle, I was bound to have Rose, and Miss Jemima would not have let her come alone."

The tone was the low, almost plaintive key, the effectiveness of which Margaret knew so well.

"'Not let her!'" The Major faced her quickly. " Margaret, she is one of those *strong-minded* women ! "

Margaret nodded brightly.

" I bet my horse she wears iron-gray curls, caught on the side of her head with tucking combs ! "

" She does," declared Margaret, her eyes dancing.

" And has a long nose — red at the end."

" Uncle, you have seen her. I *know* you have seen her," asserted Margaret, laughing up at him. " You have her very picture."

The Major groaned, and vowed that he would never survive it, and that Margaret would go down to history as the slayer of her uncle.

"I have selected my place in the grave-yard," he said, with a mournful shake of the head. "Put me close to the fence behind the raspberry thicket, where I shall be secure. Tell her there are snakes there."

"But, uncle, she is as good as gold," declared Margaret; "she is always doing good, — I believe she thinks it her mission to save the world."

The Major burst out, "That's part of this modern devilment of substituting humanitarianism for Christianity. Next thing they'll be wanting to abolish hell!"

The Major was so impressed with his peril that when Jeff, who had galloped over "for a little while," entered, announced with great ceremony by George Washington, he poured out all his apprehensions into his sympathetic ear, and it was only when he began to rally Jeff on the chance of his becoming a victim to Miss Endicott's charms, that Margaret interfered so far as to say, that Rose had any number of lovers, and one of them was "an awfully nice fellow, handsome and rich and all that." She wished "some one" would

invite him down to pay a visit in the neighborhood, for she was "afraid Rose would find
it dreadfully dull in the country." The
Major announced that he would himself make
love to her; but both Margaret and Jeff declared that Providence manifestly intended
him for Miss Jemima. He then suggested
that Miss Endicott's friend be invited to come
with her, but Margaret did not think that
would do.

"What is the name of this Paragon?" inquired Jeff.

Margaret gave his name. "Mr. Lawrence
— Pickering Lawrence."

"Why, I know him, 'Pick Lawrence.'
We were college-mates, class-mates. He used
to be in love with somebody up at his home
then; but I never identified her with your
friend. We were great cronies at the Uni-
versity. He was going to be a lawyer; but
I believe somebody died and he came into a
fortune." This history did not appear to
surprise Margaret as much as might have
been expected, and she said nothing more
about him.

About a week later Jeff took occasion to
ride over to tea, and announced that his friend

Mr. Lawrence had promised to run down and spend a few weeks with him. Margaret looked so pleased and dwelt so much on the alleged charms of the expected guest that Jeff, with a pang of jealousy, suddenly asserted that he "didn't think so much of Lawrence," that he was one of those fellows who always pretended to be very much in love with somebody, and was "always changing his clothes."

"That's what girls like," said Margaret, decisively; and this was all the thanks Jeff received.

II.

THERE was immense excitement at the Towers next day when the visitors were expected. The Major took twice his usual period to dress; George Washington with a view to steadying his nerves braced them so tight that he had great difficulty in maintaining his equipoise, and even Margaret herself was in a flutter quite unusual to one so self-possessed as she generally was. When, however, the carriage drove up to the door, the Major, with Margaret a little in advance, met the visitors at the steps in all the glory of new

blue broadcloth and flowered velvet. Sir
Charles Grandison could not have been more
elegant, nor Sir Roger more gracious. Behind him yet grander stood George — George
Washington — his master's fac-simile in ebony
down to the bandanna handkerchief and the
trick of waving the right hand in a flowing
curve. It was perhaps this spectacle which
saved the Major, for Miss Jemima was so
overwhelmed by George Washington's portentous dignity that she exhibited sufficient
humility to place the Major immediately at
his ease, and from this time Miss Jemima was
at a disadvantage, and the Major felt that he
was master of the situation.

The old lady had never been in the South
before except for a few days on the occasion
when Margaret had met her and Rose Endicott at the hotel in R——, and she had then
seen just enough to excite her inquisitiveness.
Her natural curiosity was quite amazing. She
was desperately bent on acquiring information, and whatever she heard she set down in
a journal, so as soon as she became sufficiently
acquainted with the Major she began to ply
him with questions. Her seat at table was at
the Major's right, and the questions which

she put to him proved so embarrassing, that the old gentleman declared to Margaret that if that old woman knew as much as she wanted to know she would with her wisdom eclipse Solomon and destroy the value of the Scriptures. He finally hit upon an expedient. He either traversed every proposition she suggested, or else answered every inquiry with a statement which was simply astounding. She had therefore not been at the Towers a week before she was in the possession of facts furnished by the Major which might have staggered credulity itself.

One of the many entries in her journal was to the effect that, according to Major B——, it was the custom on many plantations to shoot a slave every year, on the ground that such a sacrifice was generally salutary; that it was an expiation of past derelictions and a deterrent from repetition. And she added this memorandum:

"The most extraordinary and revolting part of it all is that this barbarous custom, which might well have been supposed confined to Dahomey, is justified by such men as Major B—— as a pious act." She inserted this query, "Can it be true?"

If she did not wholly believe the Major, she did not altogether disbelieve him. She at least was firmly convinced that it was quite possible. She determined to inquire privately of George Washington.

She might have inquired of one of the numerous maids, whose useless presence embarrassed her; but the Major foreseeing that she might pursue her investigation in other directions, had informed her that the rite was guarded with the greatest care, and that it would be as much as any one's life were worth to divulge it. Miss Jemima, therefore, was too loyal to expose one of her own sex to such danger; so she was compelled to consult George Washington, whom she believed clever enough to take care of himself.

She accordingly watched several days for an opportunity to see him alone, but without success. In fact, though she was unaware of it, George Washington had conceived for her a most violent dislike, and carefully avoided her. He had observed with growing suspicion Miss Jemima's investigation of matters relating to the estate, and her persistent pursuit of knowledge at the table had confirmed him in his idea that she contemplated the capture of his master and himself.

Like his master, he had a natural antipathy to "old women," and as the Major's threat for years had varied between "setting him free next morning" and giving him "a mistress to make him walk straight," George Washington felt that prudence demanded some vigilance on his part.

One day, under cover of the hilarity incident to the presence at dinner of Jeff and of his guest, Mr. Lawrence, Miss Jemima had pushed her inquisition even further than usual. George Washington watched her with growing suspicion, his head thrown back and his eyes half closed, and so, when, just before dinner was over, he went into the hall to see about the fire, he, after his habit, took occasion to express his opinion of affairs to the sundry members of the family who looked down at him from their dim gilt frames on the wall.

"I ain't pleased wid de way things is gwine on heah at all," he declared, poking the fire viciously and addressing his remark more particularly to an old gentlemen who in ruffles and red velvet sat with crossed legs in a high-backed chair just over the piano. "Heah me an' Marse Nat an' Miss Margaret been gittin' 'long all dese years easy an' peaceable, an'

Marse Jeff been comin' over sociable all de time, an' d' ain' been no trouble nor nuttin' till now dat ole ooman what ax mo' questions 'n a thousan' folks kin answer got to come heah and set up to Marse Nat, an' talk to him so he cyarn hardly eat." He rose from his knees at the hearth, and looking the old gentleman over the piano squarely in the face, asserted, "She got her mine sot on bein' my mistis, dat's what 'tis!" This relieved him so that he returned to his occupation of "chunking" the fire, adding, "When women sets de mines on a thing, you jes' well gin up!"

So intent was he on relieving himself of the burden on his mind that he did not hear the door softly open, and did not know any one had entered until an enthusiastic voice behind him exclaimed:

"Oh! what a profound observation!" George Washington started in much confusion; for it was Miss Jemima, who had stolen away from the table to intercept him at his task of "fixing the fires." She had, however, heard only his concluding sentence, and she now advanced with a beaming smile intended to conciliate the old butler. George Washington gave the hearth a final and hasty sweep, and

was retiring in a long detour around Miss
Jemima when she accosted him.

" Uncle George."

" Marm." He stopped and half turned.

" What a charming old place you have here ! "

George Washington cast his eye up towards
the old gentleman in the high-backed chair, as
much as to say, " You see there ? What did
I tell you ? " Then he said briefly :

" Yes, 'm."

" What is its extent ? How many acres are
there in it ? "

George Washington positively started. He
took in several of the family in his glance of
warning.

" Well, I declare, marm, I don't know,"
he began ; then it occurring to him that the
honor of the family was somehow at stake and
must be upheld, he added, " A leetle mo' 'n a
hundred thousan', marm." His exactness was
convincing. Miss Jemima threw up her hands :

" Prodigious ! How many nee — how many
persons of the African blood are there on this
vast domain ? " she inquired, getting nearer
to her point.

George, observing how much she was impressed, eyed her with rising disdain :

" Does you mean niggers, m'm? 'Bout three thousan', mum."

Another exclamation of astonishment burst from the old lady's lips.

" If you will permit me to inquire, Uncle George, how old are you?"

" She warn see if I kin wuck — dat's what she's after," said George to himself, with a confidential look at a young gentleman in a hunting dress on the wall between two windows. Then he said :

" Well, I declare, mum, you got me dyah. I ixpec' I is mos ninety years ole, I reckon I'se ol'er 'n you is — I reckon I is."

"Oh!" exclaimed Miss Jemima with a little start as if she had pricked her finger with a needle.

" Marse Nat kin tell you," continued George; " if you don't know how ole you is, all you got to do is to ax him, an' he kin tell you — he got it all set down in a book — he kin tell how ole you is to a day."

" Dear, how frightful!" exclaimed Miss Jemima, just as the Major entered somewhat hastily.

" He's a gone coon," said George Washington through the crack of the door to the old gentleman in ruffles, as he pulled the door slowly to from the outside.

The Major had left the young people in the dining-room and had come to get a book to settle a disputed quotation. He had found the work and was trying to read it without the ignominy of putting on his glasses, when Miss Jemima accosted him.

"Major, your valet appears to be a very intelligent person."

The Major turned upon her.

"My 'valet'! Madam! I have no valet!"

"I mean your body servant, your butler" — explained Miss Jemima. "I have been much impressed by him."

"George! — George Washington? — you mean George Washington! No, madam, he has not a particle of intelligence. — He is grossly and densely stupid. I have never in fifty years been able to get an idea into his head."

"Oh, dear! and I thought him so clever! I was wondering how so intelligent a person, so well informed, could be a slave."

The Major faced about.

"George! George Washington a slave! Madam, you misapprehend the situation. *He* is no slave. I am the slave, not only of him but of three hundred more as arrogant and exacting as the Czar, and as lazy as the devil!"

Miss Jemima threw up her hands in astonishment, and the Major, who was on a favorite theme, proceeded:

"Why, madam, the very coat on my back belongs to that rascal George Washington, and I do not know when he may take a fancy to order me out of it. My soul is not my own. He drinks my whiskey, steals my tobacco, and takes my clothes before my face. As likely as not he will have on this very waistcoat before the week is out."

The Major stroked his well-filled velvet vest caressingly, as if he already felt the pangs of the approaching separation.

"Oh, dear! You amaze me," began Miss Jemima.

"Yes, madam, I should be amazed myself, except that I have stood it so long. Why, I had once an affair with an intimate and valued friend, Judge Carrington. You may have heard of him, a very distinguished man! and I was indiscreet enough to carry that rascal George Washington to the field, thinking, of course, that I ought to go like a gentleman, and although the affair was arranged after we had taken our positions, and I did not have the pleasure of shooting at him, ——"

" Good heavens ! " exclaimed Miss Jemima. " *The pleasure of shooting at your friend!* Monstrous ! "

" I say I did not have that pleasure," corrected the Major, blandly; " the affair was, as I stated, arranged without a shot; yet do you know? that rascal George Washington will not allow that it was so, and I understand he recounts with the most harrowing details the manner in which ' he and I,' as he terms it, shot my friend — murdered him."

Miss Jemima gave an " Ugh. Horrible ! What depravity ! " she said, almost under her breath.

The Major caught the words.

" Yes, madam, it is horrible to think of such depravity. Unquestionably he deserves death; but what can one do ! The law, kept feeble by politicians, does not permit one to kill them, however worthless they are (he observed Miss Jemima's start,) — except, of course, by way of example, under certain peculiar circumstances, as I have stated to you." He bowed blandly.

Miss Jemima was speechless, so he pursued.

"I have sometimes been tempted to make a break for liberty, and have thought that if I could once get the rascal on the field, with my old pistols, I would settle with him which of us is the master."

"Do you mean that you would — would shoot him?" gasped Miss Jemima.

"Yes, madam, unless he should be too quick for me," replied the Major, blandly, — "or should order me from the field, which he probably would do."

The old lady turned and hastily left the room.

III.

THOUGH Miss Jemima after this regarded the Major with renewed suspicion, and confided to her niece that she did not feel at all safe with him, the old gentleman was soon on the same terms with Rose that he was on with Margaret herself. He informed her that he was just twenty-five his "last grass," and that he never could, would, or should grow a year older. He notified Jeff and his friend Mr.

Lawrence at the table that he regarded himself as a candidate for Miss Endicott's hand, and had "staked" the ground, and he informed her that as soon as he could bring himself to break an oath which he had made twenty years before, never to address another woman, he intended to propose to her. Rose, who had lingered at the table a moment behind the other ladies, assured the old fellow that he need fear no rival, and that if he could not muster courage to propose before she left, as it was leap-year, she would exercise her prerogative and propose herself. The Major, with his hand on his heart as he held the door open for her, vowed as Rose swept past him her fine eyes dancing, and her face dimpling with fun, that he was ready that moment to throw himself at her feet if it were not for the difficulty of getting up from his knees.

A little later in the afternoon Margaret was down among the rose-bushes, where Lawrence had joined her, after Rose had executed that inexplicable feminine manœuvre of denying herself to oppose a lover's request.

Jeff was leaning against a pillar, pretending to talk to Rose, but listening more to the snatches of song in Margaret's rich voice, or to the laughter which floated up to them from the garden below.

Suddenly he said abruptly, " I believe that fellow Lawrence is in love with Margaret."

Rose insisted on knowing what ground he had for so peculiar an opinion, on which he incontinently charged his friend with being one of " those fellows who falls in love with every pretty girl on whom he lays his eyes," and declared that he had done nothing but hang around Margaret ever since he had come to the county.

What Rose might have replied to this unexpected attack on one whom she reserved for her own especial torture cannot be recorded, for the Major suddenly appeared around the verandah. Both the young people instinctively straightened up.

" Ah! you rascals! I catch you!" he cried, his face glowing with jollity. "Jeff, you'd better look out, — honey catches a heap of flies, and sticks mighty hard. Rose, don't show him any mercy, — kick him, trample on him."

" I am not honey," said Rose, with a captivating look out of her bright eyes.

" Yes, you are. If you are not you are the very rose from which it is distilled."

" Oh, how charming!" cried the young lady. " How I wish some woman could hear that said to me ! "

" Don't give him credit before you hear all his proverb," said Jeff. " Do you know what he said in the dining-room ? "

" Don't credit *him* at all," replied the Major. " Don't believe him — don't listen to him. He is green with envy at my success." And the old fellow shook with amusement.

"What did he say ? Please tell me." She appealed to Jeff, and then as he was about to speak, seeing the Major preparing to run, she caught him. "No, you have to listen. Now tell me," to Jeff again.

" Well, he said honey caught lots of flies, and women lots of fools."

Rose fell back, and pointing her tapering finger at the Major, who, with mock humility, was watching her closely, declared that she would " never believe in him again." The old fellow met her with an unblushing denial of ever having made such a statement or held such traitorous sentiments, as it was, he maintained, a well established fact that flies never eat honey at all.

From this moment the Major conceived the

idea that Jeff had been caught by his fair visitor. It had never occurred to him that any one could aspire to Margaret's hand. He had thought at one time that Jeff was in danger of falling a victim to the charms of the pretty daughter of an old friend and neighbor of his, and though it appeared rather a pity for a young fellow to fall in love " out of the State," yet the claims of hospitality, combined with the fact that rivalry with Mr. Lawrence, against whom, on account of his foppishness, he had conceived some prejudice, promised a delightful excitement, more than counterbalanced that objectionable feature. He therefore immediately constituted himself Jeff's ardent champion, and always spoke of the latter's guest as " that fellow Lawrence."

Accordingly, when, one afternoon, on his return from his ride, he found Jeff, who had ridden over to tea, lounging around alone, in a state of mind as miserable as a man should be who, having come with the expectation of basking in the sunshine of Beauty's smile, finds that Beauty is out horseback riding with a rival, he was impelled to give him aid, countenance, and advice. He immediately attacked him, therefore, on his forlorn and woebegone expression, and declared that at his age he would have long ago run the game to earth, and have carried her home across his saddle-bow.

" You are afraid, sir — afraid," he asserted, hotly. " I don't know what you fellows are coming to."

Jeff admitted the accusation. "He feared," he said, " that he could not get a girl to have him." He was looking rather red when the Major cut him short.

"' Fear,' sir! Fear catches kicks, not kisses. ' Not *get* a girl to have you!' Well, upon my soul! Why don't you run after her and bawl like a baby for her to stop, whilst you get down on your knees and — *get* her to have you!"

Jeff was too dejected to be stung even by this unexpected attack. He merely said, dolorously :

" Well, how the deuce can it be done?"

"*Make* her, sir — *make* her," cried the Major. " Coerce her — compel her." The old fellow was in his element. He shook his grizzled head, and brought his hollowed hands together with sounding emphasis.

Jeff suggested that perhaps she might be impregnable, but the old fellow affirmed that no woman was this; that no fortress was too strong to be carried; that it all depended on the assailant and the vehemence of the assault; and if one did not succeed, another would. The young man brightened. His mentor, however, dashed his rising hopes by saying: "But mark this, sir, no coward can succeed. Women are rank cowards themselves, and they demand courage in their conquerors. Do you think a woman will marry a man who trembles before her? By Jove, sir! He must make her tremble!"

Jeff admitted dubiously that this sounded like wisdom. The Major burst out, "Wisdom, sir! It is the wisdom of Solomon, who had a thousand wives!"

From this time the Major constituted himself Jeff's ally, and was ready to take the field on his behalf against any and all comers. Therefore, when he came into the hall one day when Rose was at the piano, running her fingers idly over the keys, whilst Lawrence was leaning over her talking, he exclaimed:

"Hello! what treason's this? I'll tell

Jeff. He was consulting me only yesterday about —"

Lawrence muttered an objurgation; but Rose wheeled around on the piano-stool and faced him.

— "Only yesterday about the best mode of winning —" He stopped tantalizingly.

"Of winning what? I am so interested." She rose and stood just before him with a cajoling air. The Major shut his mouth tight.

"I'm as dumb as an oyster. Do you think I would betray my friend's confidence — for nothing? I'm as silent as the oracle of Delphi."

Lawrence looked anxious, and Rose followed the old man closely.

"I'll pay you anything."

"I demand payment in coin that buys youth from age." He touched his lips, and catching Rose leaned slowly forward and kissed her.

"Now, tell me — what did he say? A bargain's a bargain," she laughed as Lawrence almost ground his teeth.

"Well, he said, — he said, let me see, what did he say?" paltered the Major. "He said ie could not get a girl he loved to have him."

"Oh! did he say *that?*" She was so much interested that she just knew that Lawrence half stamped his foot.

" Yes, he said just that, and I told him —"

" Well, — what did you say?"

" Oh! I did not bargain to tell what *I* told *him*. I received payment only for betraying his confidence. If you drive a bargain I will drive one also."

Rose declared that he was the greatest old screw she ever knew, but she paid the price, and waited.

" Well? —"

"' Well?' Of course, I told him ' well.' I gave him the best advice a man ever received. A lawyer would have charged him five hundred dollars for it. I'm an oracle on heart-capture."

Rose laughingly declared she would have to consult him herself, and when the Major told her to consult only her mirror, gave him a courtesy and wished he would teach some young men of her acquaintance to make such speeches. The old fellow vowed, however, that they were unteachable; that he would as soon expect to teach young moles.

IV.

It was not more than a half hour after this when George Washington came in and found the Major standing before the long mirror, turning around and holding his coat back from his plump sides so as to obtain a fair view of his ample dimensions.

" George Washington," said he.

" Suh."

" I'm afraid I'm growing a little too stout."

George Washington walked around and looked at him with the critical gaze of a butcher appraising a fat ox.

" Oh! nor, suh, you aint, not to say *too* stout," he finally decided as the result of this inspection, " you jis gittin' sort o' potely. Hit's monsus becomin' to you."

" Do you think so?" The Major was manifestly flattered. " I was apprehensive that I might be growing a trifle fat," — he turned carefully around before the mirror, — "and from a fat old man and a scrawny old woman, Heaven deliver us, George Washington !"

" Nor, suh, you ain' got a ounce too much meat on you," said George, reassuringly;

"how much you weigh, Marse Nat, last time you was on de stilyards?" he inquired with wily interest.

The Major faced him.

"George Washington, the last time I weighed I tipped the beam at one hundred and forty-three pounds, and I had the waist of a girl."

He laid his fat hands with the finger tips touching on his round sides about where the long since reversed curves of the lamented waist once were, and gazed at George with comical melancholy.

"Dat's so," assented the latter, with wonted acquiescence. " I 'members hit well, suh, dat wuz when me and you wuz down in Gloucester tryin' to git up spunk to co'te Miss Ailsy Mann. Dat's mo'n thirty years ago."

The Major reflected. " It cannot be thirty years!—thir—ty—years," he mused.

"Yes, suh, an' better, too. 'Twuz befo' we fit de duil wid Jedge Carrington. I know dat, 'cause dat's what we shoot him 'bout—'cause he co'te Miss Ailsy an' cut we out."

"Damn your memory! Thirty years! I could dance all night then—every night in the week — and now I can hardly mount my horse without getting the thumps."

George Washington, affected by his reminiscences, declared that he had heard one of the ladies saying, "just the other day," what "a fine portly gentleman" he was.

The Major brightened.

"Did you hear that? George Washington, if you tell me a lie I'll set you free!" It was his most terrible threat, used only on occasions of exceptional provocation.

George vowed that no reward could induce him to be guilty of such an enormity, and followed it up by so skilful an allusion to the progressing youth of his master that the latter swore he was right, and that he could dance better than he could at thirty, and to prove it executed, with extraordinary agility for a man who rode at twenty stone, a *pas seul* which made the floor rock and set the windows and ornaments to rattling as if there had been an earthquake. Suddenly, with a loud "Whew," he flung himself into an arm-chair, panting and perspiring. "It's you, sir," he gasped — "you put me up to it."

"Nor, suh; tain me, Marse Nat — I's tellin' you de truf," asserted George, moved to defend himself.

"You infernal old rascal, it is you," panted the Major, still mopping his face — "you have been running riot so long you need regulation — I'll tell you what I'll do — I'll marry and give you a mistress to manage you — yes, sir, I'll get married right away. I know the very woman for you — she'll make you walk chalk!"

For thirty years this had been his threat, so George was no more alarmed than he was at the promise of being sold, or turned loose upon the world as a free man. He therefore inquired solemnly,

"Marse Nat, le' me ax you one thing — you ain' thinkin' 'bout givin' me that ole one for a mistis is you?"

"What old one, fool?" The Major stopped panting. George Washington denoted the side of his head where Miss Jemima's thin curls nestled.

"Get out of this room. Tell Dilsy to pack your chest, I'll send you off to-morrow morning."

George Washington blinked with the gravity of a terrapin. It might have been obtuseness; or it might have been silent but exquisite enjoyment which lay beneath his black skin.

"George Washington," said the Major almost in a whisper, "what made you think that?"

It was to George Washington's undying credit that not a gleam flitted across his ebony countenance as he said solemnly,

"Marse Nat, I ain say I *think* nuttin — I jis ax you, Is you? — She been meckin mighty partic'lar quiration 'bout de plantation and how many niggers we got an' all an' I jis spicionate she got her eye sort o' set on you an' me, dat's all."

The Major bounced to his feet, and seizing his hat and gloves from the table, burst out of the room. A minute later he was shouting for his horse in a voice which might have been heard a mile.

V.

JEFF laid to heart the Major's wisdom; but when it came to acting upon it the difficulty arose. He often wondered why his tongue became tied and his throat grew dry when he was in Margaret's presence these days and even just thought of saying anything serious to her. He had known Margaret ever since she was a wee bit of a baby, and had often carried her in his arms when she was a little girl and even after she grew up to be " right big." He had thought frequently of late that he would be willing to die if he might but take her in his arms. It was, therefore, with no little disquietude that he observed what he considered his friend's growing fancy for her. By the time Lawrence had taken a few strolls in the garden and a horseback ride or two with her Jeff was satisfied that he was in love with her, and before a week was out he was consumed with jealousy. Margaret was not the girl to indulge in repining on account of her lover's unhappiness. If Jeff had had a finger-ache, or had a drop of sorrow but fallen in his cup her eyes would have softened and her face would have shown how fully she felt with him ; but this — this was different. To wring his heart was a part of the business of her young ladyhood; it was a healthy process from which would come greater devotion and more loyal constancy. Then, it was so delightful to make one whom she liked as she did Jeff look so miserable. Perhaps some time she would reward him — after a long while, though. Thus, poor Jeff spent many a wretched hour cursing his fate and cursing Pick Lawrence. He thought he would create a diversion by paying desperate attention to Margaret's guest; but it resolved itself on the first opportunity into his opening his heart and confiding all his woes to her. In doing this he fell into the greatest contradiction, declaring one moment that no one suspected that he was in love with Margaret, and the next vowing that she had every reason to know he adored her, as he had been in love with her all her life. It was one afternoon in the drawing-room. Rose, with much sapience, assured him that no woman could have but one reason to know it. Jeff dolefully inquired what it was.

Rising and walking up to him she said in a mysterious whisper, —

" Tell her."

Jeff, after insisting that he had been telling her for years, lapsed into a declaration of helpless perplexity. "How can I tell her more than I have been telling her all along?" he groaned. Rose said she would show him. She seated herself on the sofa, spread out her dress and placed him behind her.

" Now, do as I tell you — no, not so, — *so;* —

now lean over, — put your arm — no, it is not necessary to touch me," as Jeff, with prompt apprehension, fell into the scheme, and declared that he was all right in a rehearsal, and that it was only in the real drama he failed. "Now say ' I love you.'" Jeff said it. They were in this attitude when the door opened suddenly and Margaret stood facing them, her large eyes opened wider than ever. She backed out and shut the door.

Jeff sprang up, his face very red.

Lawyers know that the actions of a man on being charged with a crime are by no means infallible evidence of his guilt, — but it is hard to satisfy juries of this fact. If the juries were composed of women perhaps it would be impossible.

The ocular demonstration of a man's arm around a girl's waist is difficult to explain on more than one hypothesis.

After this Margaret treated Jeff with a rigor which came near destroying the friendship of a lifetime; and Jeff became so desperate that inside of a week he had had his first quarrel with Lawrence, who· had begun to pay very devoted attention to Margaret, and as that young man was in no mood to lay balm on a bruised wound, mischief might have been done had not the Major arrived opportunely on the scene just as the quarrel came to a white-heat. It was in the hall one morning. There had been a quarrel. Jeff had just demanded satisfaction; Lawrence had just promised to afford him this peculiar happiness, and they were both glaring at each other, when the Major sailed in at the door, ruddy and smiling, and laying his hat on the table and his riding-whip across it, declared that before he would stand such a gloomy atmosphere as that created by a man's glowering looks, when there was so much sunshine just lying around to be basked in, he would agree to be "eternally fried in his own fat."

"Why, I had expected at least two affairs before this," he said jovially, as he pulled off his gloves, "and I'll be hanged if I shan't have to court somebody myself to save the honor of the family."

Jeff with dignity informed him that an affair was then brewing, and Lawrence intimated that they were both interested, when the Major declared that he would "advise the young lady to discard both and accept a soberer and a wiser man." They announced that it was a more serious affair than he had in mind, and let fall a hint of what had occurred. The Major for a moment looked gravely from one to the other, and suggested mutual explanations and retractions; but when both young men insisted that they were quite determined, and proposed to have a meeting at once, he changed. He walked over to the window and looked out for a moment. Then turned and suddenly offered to represent both parties. Jeff averred that such a proceeding was outside of the Code; this the Major gravely admitted; but declared that the affair even to this point appeared not to have been conducted in entire conformity with that incomparable system of rules, and urged that as Mr. Lawrence was a stranger and as it was desirable to have the affair conducted with as much secrecy and dispatch as possible, it might be well for them to meet as soon as convenient, and he would attend rather as a witness than as a second. The young men assented to this, and the Major, now thoroughly in earnest, with much solemnity, offered the use of his pistols, which was accepted.

In the discussion which followed, the Major took the lead, and suggested sunset that afternoon as a suitable time, and the grass-plat between the garden and the graveyard as a convenient and secluded spot. This also was agreed to, though Lawrence's face wore a soberer expression than had before appeared upon it.

The Major's entire manner had changed; his levity had suddenly given place to a gravity most unusual to him, and instead of his wonted jollity his face wore an expression of the greatest seriousness. He, after a casual glance at Lawrence, suddenly insisted that it was necessary to exchange a cartel, and opening his secretary, with much pomp proceeded to write. "You see — if things were not regular it would be butchery," he explained, considerately, to Lawrence, who winced slightly at the word. "I don't want to see you murder each other," he went on in a slow comment as he wrote, "I wish you, since you are determined to shoot — each other — to do it like — gentlemen." He took a new sheet. Suddenly he began to shout, —

"George — George Washington." There was no answer, so as he wrote on he continued to shout at intervals, "George Washington!"

After a sufficient period had elapsed for a servant crossing the yard to call to another, who sent a third to summon George, and for that functionary to take a hasty potation from a decanter as he passed through the dining-room at his usual stately pace, he appeared at the door.

"Did you call, suh?" he inquired, with that additional dignity which bespoke his recourse to the sideboard as intelligibly as if he had brought the decanters in his hand.

"Did I call!" cried the Major, without looking up. "Why don't you come when you hear me?"

George Washington steadied himself on his feet, and assumed an aggrieved expression.

"Do you suppose I can wait for you to drink all the whiskey in my sideboard? Are you getting deaf-drunk as well as blind-drunk?" he asked, still writing industriously.

George Washington gazed up at his old master in the picture on the wall, and shook his head sadly.

"Nor, suh, Marse Nat. You know I ain' drink none to git drunk. I is a member o' de church. I is full of de sperit."

The Major, as he blotted his paper, assured

him that he knew he was much fuller of it
than were his decanters, and George Washington was protesting further, when his master rose, and addressing Jeff as the challenger,
began to read. He had prepared a formal
cartel, and all the subsequent and consequen-
tial documents which appear necessary to a
well-conducted and duly bloodthirsty meeting under the duello, and he read them with
an impressiveness which was only equalled by
the portentious dignity of George Washington. As he stood balancing himself, and took
in the solemn significance of the matter, his
whole air changed; he raised his head, struck
a new attitude, and immediately assumed the
position of one whose approval of the affair
was of the utmost moment.

The Major stated that he was glad that
they had decided to use the regular duelling
pistols, not only as they were more convenient
— he having a very fine, accurate pair — but
as they were smooth bore and carried a good,
large ball, which made a clean, pretty hole,
without tearing. "Now," he explained kindly
to Lawrence, "the ball from one of these
infernal rifled concerns goes gyrating and
tearing its way through you, and makes an

orifice like a *posthole*." He illustrated his meaning with a sweeping spiral motion of his clenched fist.

Lawrence grew a shade whiter, and wondered how Jeff felt and looked, whilst Jeff set his teeth more firmly as the Major added blandly that "no gentleman wanted to blow another to pieces like a Sepoy mutineer."

George Washington's bow of exaggerated acquiescence drew the Major's attention to him.

"George Washington, are my pistols clean?" he asked.

"Yes, suh, clean as yo' shut-front," replied George Washington, grandly.

"Well, clean them again."

"Yes, suh," and George was disappearing with ponderous dignity, when the Major called him, "George Washington."

"Yes, suh."

"Tell carpenter William to come to the porch. His services may be needed," he explained to Lawrence, "in case there should be a casualty, you know."

"Yes, suh." George Washington disappeared. A moment later he re-opened the door.

" Marse Nat."

" Sir."

"Shall I send de overseer to dig de graves, suh ? "

Lawrence could not help exclaiming, " Good ——! " and then checked himself ; and Jeff gave a perceptible start.

" I will attend to that," said the Major, and George Washington went out with an order from Jeff to take the box to the office.

The Major laid the notes on his desk and devoted himself to a brief eulogy on the beautiful symmetry of " the Code," illustrating his views by apt references to a number of instances in which its absolute impartiality had been established by the instant death of both parties. He had just suggested that perhaps the two young men might desire to make some final arrangements, when George Washington reappeared, drunker and more imposing than before. In place of his ordinary apparel he had substituted a yellowish velvet waistcoat and a blue coat with brass buttons, both of which were several sizes too large for him, as they had for several years been stretched over the Major's ample person. He carried a well-worn beaver hat in his hand, which he never donned except on extraordinary occasions.

"De pistils is ready, suh," he said, in a fine voice, which he always employed when he proposed to be peculiarly effective. His self-satisfaction was monumental.

"Where did you get that coat and waistcoat from, sir?" thundered the Major. "Who told you you might have them?"

George Washington was quite taken aback at the unexpectedness of the assault, and he shuffled one foot uneasily.

"Well, you see, suh," he began, vaguely, "I know you warn' never gwine to wear 'em no mo', and seein' dat dis was a very serious recasion, an' I wuz rip-ripresentin' Marse Jeff in a jewel, I thought I ought to repear like a gent'man on dis recasion."

"You infernal rascal, didn't I tell you that the next time you took my clothes without asking my permission, I was going to shoot you?"

The Major faced his chair around with a jerk, but George Washington had in the interim recovered himself.

"Yes, suh, I remembers dat," he said, complacently, "but dat didn't have no recose to dese solemn recasions when I rip-ripresents a gent'man in de Code."

" Yes, sir, it did, I had this especially in
mind," declared the Major, unblushingly —
" I gave you fair notice, and damn me! if I
don't do it too before I'm done with you —
I'd sell you to-morrow morning if it would
not be a cheat on the man who was fool
enough to buy you. My best coat and waistcoat ! " — he looked affectionately at the gar-
ments.

George Washington evidently knew the
way to soothe him — " Who ever heah de
beat of dat ! " he said in a tone of mild complaint, partly to the young men and partly to
his old master in the ruffles and velvet over
the piano, " Marse Nat, you reckon I ain' got
no better manners 'n to teck you *bes'* coat
and weskit! Dis heah coat and weskit nuver
did you no favor anyways — I hear Miss
Marg'ret talkin' 'bout it de fust time you
ever put 'em on. Dat's de reason I tuck
'em." Having found an excuse he was as
voluble as a river — " I say to myself, I ain'
gwine let my young marster wyar dem things
no mo' roun' heah wid strange ladies an'
gent'man stayin' in de house too, — an' I so
consarned about it, I say, ' George Wash'n'n,
you got to git dem things and wyar 'em yo'-

self to keep him f'om doin' it, dat's what you got to do,' I say, and dat's de reason I tuk 'em." He looked the picture of self-sacrifice.

But the Major burst forth on him: " Why, you lying rascal, that's three different reasons you have given in one breath for taking them." At which George Washington shook his woolly head with doleful self-abnegation.

"Just look at them!" cried the Major — "My favorite waistcoat! There is not a crack or a brack in them — They look as nice as they did the day they were bought!"

This was too much for George Washington. "Dat's the favor, suh, of de pussen what has 'em on," he said, bowing grandly; at which the Major, finding his ire giving way to amusement, drove him from the room, swearing that if he did not shoot him that evening he would set him free to-morrow morning.

VI.

As the afternoon had worn away, and whilst the two principals in the affair were arranging their matters, the Major had been taking every precaution to carry out the plan for the meeting. The effect of the approaching duel upon the old gentleman was somewhat remarkable. He was in unusually high spirits; his rosy countenance wore an expression of humorous content; and, from time to time as he bustled about, a smile flitted across his face, or a chuckle sounded from the depths of his satin stock. He fell in with Miss Jemima, and related to her a series of anecdotes respecting duelling and homicide generally, so lurid in their character that she groaned over the depravity of a region where such barbarity was practised; but when he solemnly informed her that he felt satisfied from the signs of the time that some one would be shot in the neighborhood before twenty-four hours were over, the old lady determined to return home next day.

It was not difficult to secure secrecy, as the Major had given directions that no one should be admitted to the garden.

For at least an hour before sunset he had been giving directions to George Washington which that dignitary would have found some difficulty in executing, even had he remained sober; but which, in his existing condition, was as impossible as for him to change the

kinks in his hair. The Major had solemnly
assured him that if he got drunk he would
shoot him on the spot, and George Washington had as solemnly consented that he would
gladly die if he should be found in this
unprecedented condition. Immediately suc-
ceeding which, however, under the weight of
the momentous matters submitted to him, he
had, after his habit, sought aid and comfort
of his old friends, the Major's decanters, and
he was shortly in that condition when he felt
that the entire universe depended upon him.
He blacked his shoes at least twenty times,
and marched back and forth in the yard with
such portentous importance that the servants
instinctively shrunk away from his august
presence. One of the children, in their frol-
ics, ran against him; George Washington
simply said, "Git out my way," and without
pausing in his gait or deigning to look at
him, slapped him completely over.

A maid ventured to accost him jocularly to
know why he was so finely dressed. George
Washington overwhelmed her with a look of
such infinite contempt and such withering
scorn that all the other servants forthwith
fell upon her for "interferin' in Unc' George

Wash'n'ton's business." At last the Major entered the garden and bade George Washington follow him; and George Washington having paid his twentieth visit to the dining-room, and had a final interview with the liquor-case, and having polished up his old beaver anew, left the office by the side door, carrying under his arm a mahogany box about two feet long and one foot wide, partially covered with a large linen cloth. His beaver hat was cocked on the side of his head, with an air supposed to be impressive. He wore the Major's coat and flowered velvet waist-coat respecting which he had won so signal a victory in the morning, and he flaunted a large bandanna handkerchief, the ownership of which he had transferred still more recently. The Major's orders to George Washington were to convey the box to the garden in a secret manner, but George Washington was far too much impressed with the importance of the part he bore in the affair to lose the opportunity of impressing the other servants. Instead, therefore, of taking a by-path, he marched ostentatiously through the yard with a manner which effected his object, if not his master's, and which struck the entire circle of servants with inexpressible awe. However, after he gained the garden and reached a spot where he was no longer in danger of being observed by any one, he adopted a manner of the greatest secrecy, and proceeded to the place selected for the meeting with a degree of caution which could not have been greater had he been covertly stealing his way through a band of hostile Indians. The spot chosen for the meeting was a grass plot bounded on three sides by shrubbery and on the fourth by the wall of the little square within which had been laid to rest the mortal remains of some half dozen generations of the Burwells. Though the grass was green and the sky above was of the deep steely hue which the late afternoon brings; yet the thick shrubbery which secluded the place gave it an air of wildness, and the tops of the tall monuments gleaming white over the old wall against the dark cedars, added an impression of ghostliness which had long caused the locality to be generally avoided by the negroes from the time that the afternoon shadows began to lengthen.

George Washington, indeed, as he made his way stealthily down towards the rendezvous glanced behind him once or twice as if he were not at all certain that some impalpable pursuer were not following him, and he almost jumped out of his shoes when the Major, who had for ten minutes been pacing up and down the grass-plat in a fume of impatience, caught sight of him and suddenly shouted, "Why don't you come on, you — rascal?"

As soon as George Washington recognized that the voice was not supernatural, he recovered his courage and at once disarmed the Major, who, watch in hand, was demanding if he supposed he had nothing else to do than to wait for him all night, by falling into his vein and acquiescing in all that he said in abuse of the yet absent duellists, or at least of one of them.

He spoke in terms of the severest reprobation of Mr. Lawrence, declaring that he had never had a high opinion of his courage, or, indeed, of any quality which he possessed. He was, perhaps, not quite prepared to join in an attack on Jeff, of whose frequent benefactions he entertained a lively recollection amounting to gratitude, at least in the accepted French idea of that virtue, and as he

had constituted himself Jeff's especial representative for this "solemn recasion," he felt
a personal interest in defending him to some
extent.

At last the Major ordered him to take out
the weapons and some little time was spent
in handling them, George Washington exam-
ining them with the air of a connoisseur.
The Major asserted that he had never seen a
prettier spot, and George Washington, immediately striking an attitude, echoed the sentiment. He was, indeed, so transported with
its beauty that he declared it reminded him of
the duel he and the Major fought with Judge
Carrington, which he positively declared, was
"a jewel like you been read about," and he
ended with the emphatic assertion, " Ef dese
gent'mens jes plump each urr like we did de
Judge dat evelin ! —— " A wave of the hand
completed the period.

The Major turned on him with a positive
denial that he had ever even shot at the
Judge, but George Washington unblushingly
insisted that they had, and in fact had shot
him twice. "We hit him fyah an' squar'."
He levelled a pistol at a tree a few yards distant, and striking an attitude, squinted along

the barrel with the air of an old hand at the weapon.

The Major reiterated his statement and recalled the fact that, as he had told him and others a thousand times, they had shaken hands on the spot, which George Washington with easy ad ptability admitted, but claimed that "ef he hadn't 'a'shook hands we'd 'a'shot him, sho! Dis here gen+'man ain' gwine git off quite so easy," he declared, having already decided that Lawrence was to experience the deadly accuracy of his and Jeff's aim. He ended with an unexpected "Hic!" and gave a litt'. lurch, ..hi h betrayed his condition, but immediately gathered himself together again.

The M jor looked at him quizzically as he stood pistols in hand in all the grandeur of his assumed character. The shadow of disappointment at the non-appearance of the duellists which had rested on his round face, passed away, and he suddenly asked him which way he thought they had better stand. George Washington twisted his head on one side and, after striking a deliberative attitude and looking the plat well over, gave his judgment.

"Ah—so," said the Major, and bade him step off ten paces.

George Washington cocked his hat considerably more to the side, and with a wave of his hand, caught from the Major, took ten little mincing steps; and without turning, glanced back over his shoulder and inquired, " Ain' dat mighty fur apart ? "

The Major stated 'hat it was necessary to give them some chance. And this appeared to satisfy him, for he admitted, " Yas, suh, dat's so, dee 'bleeged to have a chance," and immediately marked a point a yard or more short of that to which he had stepped.

The Major then announced that he would load the pistols without waiting for the advent of the other gentlemen, as he "represented both of them."

This was too much for so accomplished an adept at the Code as George Washington, and he immediately asserted that such a thing was preposterous, asking with some scorn, as he stru'ted up and down, " Who ever heah o' one gent'man ripresentin' two in a jewel, Marse Nat ? "

The Major bowed politely. " I was afraid it was a little incompatible," he said.

" Of cose it's incomfatible," said George Washington. " I ripresents one and you de t'urr. Dat's de way! I ripresents *Marse Jeff*. I know *he* ain' gwine fly de track. I done know him from a little lad. Dat urr gent'man I ain' know nuttin tall about. You ripresents him." He waved his hand in scorn.

"Ah!" said the Major, as he set laboriously about loading the pistols, handling the balls somewhat ostentatiously.

George Washington asserted, "I b'lieve I know mo' 'bout the Code 'n you does, Marse Nat."

The Major looked at him quizzically as he rammed the ball down hard. He was so skilful that George at length added condescendingly, "But I see you ain' forgit how to handle dese things."

The Major modestly admitted, as he put on a cap, that he used to be a pretty fair shot, and George Washington in an attitude as declarative of his pride in the occasion as his inebriated state admitted, was looking on with an expression of supreme complacency, when the Major levelled the weapon and sighted along its barrel. George Washington gave a jump which sent his cherished beaver bouncing twenty feet.

"Look out, Marse Nat! Don' handle dat thing so keerless, please, suh."

The Major explained that he was just trying its weight, and declared that it " came up
beautifully ; " to which George Washington
after he had regained his damaged helmet
assented with a somewhat unsteady voice.
The Major looked at his watch and up at the
trees, the tops of which were still brightened
with the reflection from the sunset sky, and
muttered an objurgation at the failure of the
principals to appear, vowing that he never
before knew of a similar case, and that at
least he had not expected Jeff to fail to come
to time.   George Washington again proudly
announced that he represented Jeff and that
it was " that urr gent'man what had done fly
de track, that urr gent'man what you ripresents, Marse Nat."   He spoke with unveiled
contempt.

The Major suddenly turned on him.

" George Washington ! "

" Suh ! "   He faced him.

" If my principal fails to appear, I must
take his place.   The rule is, the second takes
the place of his non-appearing principal."

" In cose dat's de rule," declared George
Washington as if it were his own suggestion ;
" de secon' tecks de place o' de non-repearin'

sprinciple, and dat's what mecks me say what I does, dat man is done run away, suh, dat's what's de motter wid him. He's jes' natchelly skeered. He couldn' face dem things, suh." He nodded towards the pistols, his thumbs stuck in the armholes of his flowered velvet vest. As the Major bowed George Washington continued with a hiccough, "He ain' like we gent'mens whar's ust to 'em an' don' mine 'em no mo' 'n pop-crackers."

"George Washington," said the Major, solemnly, with his eyes set on George Washington's velvet waistcoat, "take your choice of these pistols."

The old duellist made his choice with due deliberation. The Major indicated with a wave of his hand one of the spots which George had marked for the expected duellists. "Take your stand there, sir." George Washington marched grandly up and planted himself with overwhelming dignity, whilst the Major, with the other pistol in his hand, quietly took his stand at the other position, facing him.

"George," he said, "George Washington."

"Suh." George Washington was never so imposing.

"My principal, Mr. Pickering Lawrence, having failed to appear at the designated time and place to meet his engagement with Mr. Jefferson Lewis, I, as his second and representative, offer myself to take his place and assume any and all of his obligations."

George Washington bowed grandly.

"Yes, suh, of cose, — dat is accordin' to de Code," he said with solemnity befitting the occasion.

The Major proceeded.

"And your principal, Mr. Jefferson Lewis, having likewise failed to appear at the proper time, you take his place."

"Suh," ejaculated George Washington, in sudden astonishment, turning his head slightly as if he were not certain he had heard correctly, "Marse Nat, jis say dat agin, please, suh?"

The Major elevated his voice and advanced his pistol slightly.

"I say, your principal, Mr Jefferson Lewis, having in like manner failed to put in his appearance at the time and place agreed on for the meeting, you as his representative take his place and assume all his obligations."

"Oh! nor, suh, I don't!" exclaimed George Washington, shaking his head so violent¹

that the demoralized beaver fell off again and
rolled around unheeded. "I ain' bargain for
no sich thing as dat. Nor, suh!"

But the Major was obdurate.

"Yes, sir, you do. When you accept the
position of second, you assume all the obligations attaching to that position, and —— " the
Major advanced his pistol — "I shall shoot at
you."

George Washington took a step towards
him. "Oh! goodness! Marse Nat, you ain'
gwine do nuttin like dat, is you!" His jaw
had fallen, and when the Major bowed with
deep solemnity and replied, "Yes, sir, and you
can shoot at me," he burst out.

"Marse Nat, I don' warn' shoot at you.
What I warn' shoot at you for? I ain' got
nuttin 'ginst you on de fatal uth. You been
good master to me all my days an' —— " The
Major cut short this sincere tribute to his vir-
tues, by saying: "Very well, you can shoot
or not as you please. I shall aim at that
waistcoat." He raised his pistol and partially closed one eye. George Washington
dropped on his knees.

"Oh, Marse Nat, please, suh. What you
want to shoot me for? Po' ole good-for-

nuttin George Washington, whar ain' nuver done you no harm" (the Major's eye glanced over his blue coat and flowered vest; George saw it), " but jes steal you' whiskey an' you' clo'es an' — Marse Nat, ef you le' me off dis time I oon nuver steal no mo' o' you' clo'es, er you' whiskey, er nuttin. Marse Nat, you wouldn' shoot po' ole good-for-nuttin George Washington, whar fotch' up wid you?"

"Yes, sir, I would," declared the Major, sternly. "I am going to give the word, and —" he raised the pistol once more.

George Washington began to creep toward him. "Oh, Lordy! Marse Nat, please, suh, don' pint dat thing at me dat away — hit's loaded! Oh, Lordy!" he shouted. The Major brandished his weapon fiercely.

"Stand up, sir, and stop that noise — one — two — three," he counted, but George Washington was flat on the ground.

"Oh, Marse Nat, please, suh, don't. I'se feared o' dem things." A sudden idea struck him. "Marse Nat, you is about to loss a mighty valuable nigger," he pleaded; but the Major simply shouted to him to stand up and not disgrace the gentleman he represented. George Washington seized on the word; it was his firfal hope.

"Marse Nat, I don't ripresent nobody, suh, nobody at all, suh. I ain' nuttin but a good-for-nuttin, wuthless nigger, whar brung de box down heah cuz you tole me to, suh, dat's all. An' I'll teck off you' coat an' weskit dis minit ef you'll jis le' me git up off de groun', suh." Jeff suddenly appeared. George lay spraddled out on the ground as flat as a field lark, but at Jeff's appearance, he sprang behind him. Jeff, in amazement, was inquiring the meaning of all the noise he had heard, when Lawrence appeared on the scene. The Major explained briefly.

"It was that redoubtable champion bellowing. As our principals failed to appear on time, he being an upholder of the Code, suggested that we were bound to take the places respectively of those we represented —— "

"Nor, suh, I don' ripresent nobody," interrupted George Washington; but at a look from the Major he dodged again behind Jeff. The Major, with his eye on Lawrence, said:

"Well, gentlemen, let's to business. We have but a few minutes of daylight left. I presume you are ready?"

Both gentlemen bowed, and the Major proceeded to explain that he had loaded both pistols himself with precisely similar charges, and that they were identical in trigger, sight, drift, and weight, and had been tested on a number of occasions, when they had proved to be "excellent weapons and remarkably accurate in their fire." The young men bowed silently; but when he turned suddenly and called "George Washington," that individual nearly jumped out of his coat. The Major ordered him to measure ten paces, which, after first giving notice that he "didn't ripresent nobody," he proceeded to do, taking a dozen or more gigantic strides, and hastily retired again behind the safe bulwark of Jeff's back. As he stood there in his shrunken condition, he about as much resembled the pompous and arrogant duellist of a half-hour previous as a wet and bedraggled turkey does the strutting, gobbling cock of the flock. The Major, with an objurgation at him for stepping "as if he had on seven league boots," stepped off the distance himself, explaining to Lawrence that ten paces was about the best distance, as it was sufficiently distant to "avoid the unpleasantness of letting a gentleman feel that he was within touching distance," and yet "near enough to avoid useless mutilation."

Taking out a coin, he announced that he would toss up for the choice of position, or rather would make a "disinterested person" do so, and, holding out his hand, he called George Washington to toss it up. There was no response until the Major shouted, "George Washington, where are you — you rascal!"

"Heah me, suh," said George Washington, in a quavering voice, rising from the ground, where he had thrown himself to avoid any stray bullets, and coming slowly forward, with a pitiful, "Please, suh, don' p'int dat thing dis away."

The Major gave him the coin, with an order to toss it up, in a tone so sharp that it made him jump; and he began to turn it over nervously in his hand, which was raised a little above his shoulder. In his manipulation it slipped out of his hand and disappeared. George Washington in a dazed way looked in his hand, and then on the ground. "Hi! whar' hit?" he muttered, getting down on his knees and searching in the grass. "Dis heah place is evil-sperited."

The Major called to him to hurry up, but he was too intent on solving the problem of the mysterious disappearance of the quarter.

"I ain' nuver like dis graveyard bein' right heah," he murmured. "Marse Nat, don' you have no mo' to do wid dis thing."

The Major's patience was giving out. "George Washington, you rascal!" he shouted, "do you think I can wait all night for you to pull up all the grass in the garden? Take the quarter out of your pocket, sir!"

"'Tain' in my pocket, suh,'" quavered George Washington, feeling there instinctively, however, when the coin slipped down his sleeve into his hand again. This was too much for him. "Hi! befo' de king," he exclaimed, "how it git in my pocket? Oh, Marster! de devil is 'bout heah, sho'! Marse Nat, you fling it up, suh. I ain' nuttin but a po' sinful nigger. Oh, Lordy!" And handing over the quarter tremulously, George Washington flung himself flat on the ground and, as a sort of religious incantation, began to chant in a wild, quavering tone the funeral hymn:

"Hark! from the tombs a doleful sound."

The Major tossed up and posted the duellists, and with much solemnity handed them the pistols, which both the two young men received quietly. They were pale, but perfectly steady. The Major then asked them, " Gentlemen, are you ready ? " whilst at the omnious sound George Washington's voice in tremulous falsetto, struck in,

" Ye-ee—so-ons off meenn co-ome view-ew the-ee groun',
Wher-ere you-ou m—uss' shor-ort-ly lie."

They announced themselves ready just as George Washington, looking up from the ground, where he, like the " so-ons off meenn," was lying, discovered that he was not more than thirty yards out of the line of aim, and with a muttered " Lordy!" began to crawl away.

There was a confused murmur from the direction of the path which led to the house, and the Major shouted, " Fire — one — two — three."

Both young men, facing each other and looking steadily in each other's eyes, with simultaneous action fired their pistols into the air.

At the report a series of shrieks rang out from the shrubbery towards the house, whilst George Washington gave a wild yell and began to kick like a wounded bull, bellowing that he was " killed — killed."

The Major had just walked up to the duellists, and, relieving them of their weapons, had with a comprehensive wave of the hand congratulated them on their courage and urged them to shake hands, which they were in the act of doing, when the shrubbery parted and Margaret, followed closely by Rose and by Miss Jemima panting behind, rushed in upon them, crying at the tops of their voices, " Stop ! Stop !"

The two young ladies addressed themselves respectively to Jeff and Lawrence, and both were employing all their eloquence when Miss Jemima appeared. Her eye caught the prostrate form of George Washington, who lay flat on his face kicking and groaning at intervals. She pounced upon the Major with so much vehemence that he was almost carried away by the sudden onset.

" Oh ! You wretch ! What have you done ?" she panted, scarcely able to articulate.

"Done, madam ?" asked the Major, gravely.

" Yes ; what have you done to *that* poor miserable creature — *there !* " She actually seized the Major and whirled him around with one hand, whilst with the other she pointed at the prostrate and now motionless George Washington.

" What have I been doing with him ? "

" Yes, with *him*. Have you been carrying out your barbarous rite on his inoffensive person !" she gasped.

The Major's eye lit up.

" Yes, madam," he said, taking up one of the pistols, " and I rejoice that you are here to witness its successful termination. George Washington has been selected as the victim this year; his monstrous lies, his habitual drunken worthlessness, his roguery, culminating in the open theft to-day of my best coat and waistcoat, marked him naturally as the proper sacrifice. I had not the heart to cheat any one by selling him to him. I was therefore constrained to shoot him. He was, with his usual triflingness, not killed at the first fire, although he appears to be dead. I will now finish him by putting a ball into his back ; observe the shot." He advanced, and cocking the pistol, " click — click," stuck it carefully in the middle of George Washington's fat back. Miss Jemima gave a piercing shriek and flung herself on the Major to seize the pistol; but she might have spared herself;

for George Washington suddenly bounded from the ground and, with one glance at the levelled weapon, rushed crashing through the shrubbery, followed by the laughter of the young people, the shrieks of Miss Jemima, and the shouts of the Major for him to come back and let him kill him.

That evening, when Margaret, seated on the Major's knee, was rummaging in his vest pockets for any loose change which might be there (which by immemorial custom belonged to her), she suddenly pulled out two large, round bullets. The Major seized them; but it was too late. When, however, he finally obtained possession of them he presented them to Miss Jemima, and solemnly requested her to preserve them as mementoes of George Washington's miraculous escape.

I HAD the good fortune to come from " the
old county of Hanover," as that particular
division of the State of Virginia is affectionately called by nearly all who are so lucky as
to have first seen the light amid its broom-
straw fields and heavy forests; and to this
happy circumstance I owed the honor of a
special visit from one of its most loyal citi-
zens. Indeed, the glories of his native county
were so embalmed in his memory and were
so generously and continuously imparted to
all his acquaintances, that he was in the
county of his adoption universally known
after an absence of forty years as " Old Hanover." I had not been long in F—— when
I was informed that I might, in right of
the good fortune respecting my birthplace,
to which I have referred, expect a visit from
my distinguished fellow-countyman, and thus
I was not surprised, when one afternoon a
message was brought in that "Ole Hanover

was in the yard, and had called to pay his
bes' bespecks to de gent'man what hed de
honor to come f'om de ole county."

I immediately went out, followed by my
host, to find that the visit was attended with
a formality which raised it almost to the
dignity of a ceremonial. "Old Hanover"
was accompanied by his wife, and was attended by quite a number of other negroes,
who had followed him either out of curiosity
excited by the importance he had attached to
the visit, or else in the desire to shine in
reflected glory as his friends. "Old Hanover" himself stood well out in front of the
rest, like an old African chief in state with
his followers behind him about to receive an
embassy. He was arrayed with great care,
in a style which I thought at first glance was
indicative of the clerical calling, but which I
soon discovered was intended to be merely
symbolical of approximation to the dignity
which was supposed to pertain to that profes-
sion. He wore a very long and baggy coat
which had once been black, but was now
tanned by exposure to a reddish brown, a
vest which looked as if it had been velvet
before the years had eaten the nap from it,

and changed it into a fabric not unlike leather. His shirt was obviously newly washed for the occasion, and his high clean collar fell over an ample and somewhat bulging white cloth, which partook of the qualities of both stock and necktie. His skin was of that lustrous black which shines as if freshly oiled, and his face was closely shaved except for two tufts of short, white hair, one on each side, which shone like snow against his black cheeks. He wore an old and very quaint beaver, and a pair of large, old-fashioned, silver-rimmed spectacles, which gave him an air of portentous dignity.

When I first caught sight of him, he was leaning on a long hickory stick, which might have been his staff of state, and his face was set in an expression of superlative importance. As I appeared, however, he at once removed his hat, and taking a long step forward, made me a profound bow. I was so much impressed by him, that I failed to catch the whole of the grandiloquent speech with which he greeted me. I had evidently secured his approval; for he boldly declared that he " would 'a' recognizated me for one of de rail quality cf he had foun' me in a cuppen." I was immediately conscious of the effect which his endorsement produced on his companions. They regarded me with new interest, if any expression so bovine deserved to be thus characterized.

"I tell dese folks up heah dee don't know nuthin' 'bout rail quality," he asserted with a contemptuous wave of his arm, which was manifestly intended to embrace the entire section in its comprehensive sweep. "Dee 'ain' nuver had no 'quaintance wid it," he explained, condescendingly. His friends accepted this criticism with proper submissiveness.

"De Maconses, de Berkeleyses, de Carterses, de Bassettses, de Wickhamses, de Nelsonses, an' dem!"—(the final ending "es" was plainly supposed to give additional dignity)—"now *dee* is sho 'nough quality. I know all 'bout 'em." He paused long enough to permit this to sink in.

"I b'longst to Doc' Macon. *You* know what *he* wuz?"

His emphasis compelled me to acknowledge his exalted position or abandon forever all hope of retaining my own; so I immediately assented, and inquired how long he had been in "this country," as he designated his adopted region. He turned with some severity to one of his companions, a stout and slatternly woman, very black, and many years his junior.

"How long is I been heah, Lucindy?"

The woman addressed, by way of answer, turned half away, and gave a little nervous laugh. "I don't know how long you been heah, you been heah so long; mos' forty years, I reckon." This sally called from her companions a little ripple of amusement.

"Dat's my wife, suh," the old gentleman explained, apologetically. "She's de one I got now; she come f'om up heah in dis kentry." His voice expressed all that the words were intended to convey. Lucindy, who appeared accustomed to such contemptuous reference, merely gave another little explosion which shook her fat shoulders.

As, however, I was expected to endorse all his views, I changed the embarrassing subject by inquiring how he had happened to leave the old county.

"Ole marster gi' me to Miss Fanny when she ma'yed Marse William Fitzhugh," he explained. "I wuz ma'yed den to Marth' Ann; she wuz Miss Fanny's maid, an' when she come up heah wid Miss Fanny, I recompany her." He would not admit that his removal was a permanent one. " I al'ays layin' out to go back home, but I 'ain' been yit. Dee's mos' all daid b'fo' dis, suh?"

He spoke as if this were a fact, but there was a faint inquiry in his eyes if not in his tone. I was sorry not to be able to inform him differently, and, to change the subject, I started to ask him a question. "Martha Ann—" I began, and then paused irresolute.

"She's daid too," he said simply.

" How many children have you?" I asked.

" I 'ain' got but beah one now, suh, ef I got dat one," he replied; " dat's P'laski."

" How many have you had?"

" Well, suh, dat's a partic'lar thing to tell," he said, with a whimsical look on his face. " De Scripturs says you is to multiply an' replanish de uth; but I s'pecks I's had some several mo'n my relowance; dar's Jeems, an' Peter, an' Jeremiah, an' Hezekiah, an' Zekyel, Ananias an' Malachi, Matthew an' Saint Luke, besides de gals. Dee's all gone; an' now I 'ain' got but jes dat P'laski. He's de wuthlisses one o' de whole gang. He tecks after his mammy."

The reference to Pulaski appeared to occasion some amusement among his friends, and I innocently inquired if he was Martha Ann's son.

"Nor, *suh, dat* he warn'!" was the vehement and indignant answer. "Ef he had 'a' been, he nuver would 'a' got me into all dat trouble. Dat wuz de mortification o' my life, suh. He got all dat meanness f'om his mammy. Dat ooman dyah is his mammy." He indicated the plump Lucindy with his long stick, which he poked at her contemptuously. "Dat's what I git for mar'yin' one o' dese heah up-kentry niggers!" The "up-kentry" spouse was apparently quite accustomed to this characterization, for she simply looked away, rather in embarrassment at my gaze being directed to her than under any stronger emotion. Her liege continued: "Lucindy warn' quality like me an' Marth' Ann, an' her son tooken after her. What's in de myah will come out in de colt; an' he is de meanes' chile I uver had. I name de urrs f'om de Scriptur', but he come o' a diff'- ent stock, an' I name him arter Mr. P'laski Greener, whar Lucindy use' to b'longst to, an' I reckon maybe dat's de reason he so

natchally evil. I had mo' trouble by recount
o' dat boy 'n I hed when I los' Marth' Ann."

The old fellow threw back his head and
gave a loud " Whew ! " actually removing his
large spectacles in his desperation at Pulaski's
wickedness. Again there was a suppressed
chuckle from his friends ; so, seeing that
some mystery attached to the matter, I put a
question which started him.

" Well, I'll tell you, suh," he began. " Hit
all growed out of a tunament, suh. You an'
I knows all discerning tunaments, 'cuz we
come f'om de ole county o' Hanover, whar
de *raise* tunaments " — (he referred to them
as if they had been a species of vegetables)
— " but we 'ain' nuver hearn de modification
of a *nigger* ridin' in a tunament ? "

I admitted this, and, after first laying his
hat carefully on the ground, he proceeded :

" Well, you know, suh, dat P'laski got de
notionment in he haid dat he wuz to ride in
a tunament. He got dat f'om dat ooman."
He turned and pointed a trembling finger at
his uncomplaining spouse ; and then slowly
declared, " Lord ! I wuz outdone dat day."

I suggested that possibly he had not followed Solomon's injunction as rigidly as

Pulaski's peculiar traits of character had demanded; but he said promptly:

" Yes, suh, I did. I whupped him faithful; but he took whuppin' like a ole steer. Hickory didn' 'pear to have no 'feck on him. He didn' had no memory; he like a ole steer: got a thick skin an' a short memory; he wuz what I call one o' dese disorde'ly boys."

He paused long enough to permit this term, taken from the police court reports, to make a lodgement, and then proceeded:

" He wuz so wuthless at home, I hired him out to ole Mis' Twine for fo' dollars an' a half a mont' — an' more'n he wuth, too! — to see ef po' white ooman kin git any wuck out'n him. A po' white ooman kin git wuck out a nigger ef anybody kin, an' 'twuz down dyah that he got had foolishness lodgicated in he haid. You see, ole Mis' Twine warn' so fur f'om Wash'n'n. Nigger think ef he kin git to Wash'n'n, he done got in heaven. Well, I hire him to ole Mis' Twine, 'cuz I think she'll keep P'laski straight, an' ef I don' git but one fo' dollars an' a half f'om him, hit's dat much; but 'pear like he got to runnin' an' consortin' wid some o' dem urr free-issue niggers roun' dyah, an' dee larne him mo' foolishness'n I think dee able; 'cuz a full hawg cyarn drink no mo'."

The old fellow launched out into diatribes against the "free issues," who, he declared, expected to be "better than white folks, like white folks ain' been free sense de wull begin." He, however, shortly returned to his theme.

"Well, fust thing I knowed, one Sunday I wuz settin' down in my house, an' heah come P'laski all done fixed up wid a high collar on, mos' high as ole master's, an' wid a better breeches on 'n I uver wear in my *life*, an' wid a creevat! an' a cane! an' wid a seegar! He comes in de do' an' hol' he seegar in he han', sort o' so " (illustrating), "an' he teck off he hat kine o' flourishy 'whurr,' an' say, 'Good mornin', pa an' ma.' He mammy — *dat* she — monsus pleaged wid dem manners; she ain' know no better; but I ain' nuver like nobody to gobble roun' *me*, an' I say, 'Look heah, boy, don' fool wid me; I ain' feelin' well to-day, an' ef you fool wid me, when I git done wid you, you oon feel well you'self.' Den he kine o' let he feathers down; an' presney he say he warn me to len' him three dollars an' a half. I ax him what

he warn do wid it, 'cuz I know I ain' gwine
len' to him — jes well len' money to a mus'-
rat hole; — an' he say he warn it for a tunament. 'Hi!' I say, 'P'laski, what air a tunament?' I mecked out, you see, like I ain'
recognizated what he meck correspondence
to; an' he start to say, 'A tunament, pa —'
but I retch for a barrel hoop whar layin' by
kine o' amiable like, an' he stop, like young
mule whar see mud-puddle in de road, an'
say, 'A tunament — a tunament is whar you
gits 'pon a hoss wid a pole, an' rides hard as
you kin, an' pokes de pole at a ring, an' —'
When he gets right dyah, I interrup's him,
an' I say, 'P'laski,' says I, 'I's raised wid
de fust o' folks, 'cuz I's raised wid de Maconses at Doc' Macon's in Hanover, an' I's
spectated fish fries, an' festibals, an' bobby-
cues; but I ain' nuver witness nuttin' like
dat — a nigger ridin' 'pon a hoss hard as he
kin stave, an' nominatin' of it a tunament,' I
says. 'You's talkin' 'bout a hoss-race,' I says,
' 'cuz dat's de on'yes' thing,' I says, 'a nigger
rides in.' You know, suh," he broke in suddenly, "you and I's seen many a hoss-race,
'cuz we come f'om hoss kentry, right down
dyah f'om whar Marse Torm Doswell live,

an' we done see hoss-races whar wuz hoss-races sho 'nough, at the ole Fyarfiel' race-co'se, whar hosses used to run could beat buds flyin' an' so I tole him. I tole him I nuver heah nobody but a po' white folks' nigger call a hoss-race a tunament; an' I tole him I reckon de pole he talkin' 'bout wuz de hick'ry dee used to tune de boys' backs wid recasionally when dee didn' ride right. Dat cut him dowr might'ly, 'cuz dat ermine him o' de hick'ries I done wyah out 'pon him; but he say, 'Nor, 'tis a long pole whar you punch th'oo a ring, an' de one whar punch de moes, he crown de queen.' I tole him dat de on'yes' queen I uver heah 'bout wuz a cow ole master had, whar teck de fust prize at de State fyah in Richmond one year; but he presist dat this wuz a tunament queen, and he warn three dollars an' a half to get him a new shut an' to pay he part ov de supper. Den I tole him ef he think I gwine give him three dollars an' a half for dat foolishness he mus' think I big a fool as he wuz. Wid dat he begin to act kine o' aggervated, which I teck for impidence, 'cuz I nuver could abeah chillern ner women to be sullen roun' me; an' I gi' him de notification dat ef I cotch him foolin' wid

any tunament I gwine ride him tell he oon
know wherr he ain't a mule hisself; an' I
gwine have hick'ry pole dyah too. Den I tolt
him he better go 'long back to ole Mis' Twine,
whar I done hire him to; an' when he see
me pick up de barrel hoop an' start to roll up
my sleeve, he went; an' I heah he jine dat
Jim Sinkfiel', an' dat's what git me into all
dat tribilation."

"What got you in?" I inquired, in some
doubt as to his meaning.

"Dat tunament, suh. P'laski rid it! An'
what's mo,' suh, he won de queen, — one o'
ole man Bob Sibley's impident gals, — an'
when he come to crown her, he crown her
wid ole Mis' Twine's weddin'-ring!"

There was a subdued murmur of amusement in the group behind him, and I could
not but inquire how he came to perform so
extraordinary a ceremony.

"Dat I don' know, suh; but so 'twair.
Fust information I had on it wuz when I went
down to ole Mis' Twine's to get he mont's
weges. I received de ontelligence on de way
dat he had done lef' dyah, an' dat ole Mis'
Twine gol' ring had lef' by de same road at
de same time. Dat correspondence mortify me

might'ly' cuz I hadn' raised P'laski no sich a
ways as dat. He was dat ooman's son to be
sho' an' I knowed he wuz wuthless, but still I
hadn' respect him to steal ole Mis' Twine weddin'-ring, whar she wyah on her finger ev'y
day, an' whar wuz gol' too. I want de infi-
mation 'bout de fo' dollars an' a half, so I
went 'long; but soon as ole Mis' Twine see
me she began to quoil. I tell her I just
come to git de reasonment o' de matter, an' I
'ain' got nuthin' 'tall to say 'bout P'laski.
Dat jes like bresh on fire; she wuss'n befo'.
She so savigrous I tolt her I 'ain' nuver had
nobody to prevaricate nuttin' 'bout me; dat
I b'longst to Doc' Macon, o' Hanover, an' I
ax her ef she knowed de Maconses. She say,
nor, she 'ain' know 'em, nor she ain' nuver
hearn on 'em, an' she wished shé hadn' nuver
hearn on me an' my thievin' boy — dat's
P'laski. Well, tell then, I mighty consarned
'bout P'laski; but when she said she 'ain'
nuver hearn on the Maconses, I ain' altogether b'lieve P'laski done teck her ring,
cause I ain' know whether she got any ring;
though I know sence the tunament he mean
enough for anything; an' I tolt her so, an' I
tolt her I wuz raised wid quality — sence she

ain' know the Maconses, I ain' tole her no mo' 'bout dem, 'cuz de Bible say you is not to cast pearls befo' hawgs — an' dat I had tote de corn-house keys many a time, an' Marth' Ann used to go in ole Mistis' trunks same as ole Mistis herself. Right dyah she mought 'a' cotch me ef she had knowed that P'laski warn' Marth' Ann's son; but she ain' know de Maconses, an' in cose she ain' 'quainted wid de servants, so she don' know it. Well, suh, she rar an' she pitch. Yo' nuver heah a ooman talk so befo' in yo' life; an' fust thing I knew she gone in de house, she say she gwine git a gun an' run me off dat lan'. But I ain' wait for dat: don nobody have to git gun to run me off dee lan'. I jes teck my foot in my han' an' come 'long way by myself, 'cuz I think maybe a ooman 'at could cuss like a man mout shoot like a man too."

"Where did you go and what did you do next?" I asked the old fellow as he paused with a whimsical little nod of satisfaction at his wisdom.

"I went home, suh," he said. "I heah on de way dat P'laski had sho 'nough done crownt Bob Sibly's gal, Lizzy Susan, wid de ring, an' dat he wuz gwine to Wash'n'n, but wuz done

come home to git some things b'fo' he went;
so I come straight 'long behinst him jes swif'
as my foot could teck me. I didn' was'e
much time," he said, with some pride, "'cuz
he had done mighty nigh come gittin' me
shot. I jes stop long 'nough to cut me a
bunch o' right keen hick'ries, an' I jes come
'long shakin' my foot. When I got to my
house I ain' fine nobody dyah but Lucindy —
dat ve'y ooman dyah" — pointing his long
stick at her — "an' I lay my hick'ries on de
bed, an' ax her is she see P'laski. Fust she
meck out dat she ain' lreah me, she so induschus; I nuver see her so induschus; but
when I meck 'quiration agin she bleeged
to answer me, an' she 'spon' dat she 'ain'
see him; 'cuz she see dat my blood wuz
up, an' she know dee wuz trouble 'pendin' for
P'laski. Dat worry me might'ly, an' I say,
'Lucindy, ef you is done meck dat boy resent
hisself f'om heah, you is done act like a po'
white folks' nigger,' I say, 'an' you's got to
beah de depravity o' his transgression.' When
I tolt her dat she nuver got mad, 'cuz she
know she air not quality like me an' Marth'
Ann; but she 'pear right smartly disturbed,
an' she 'clar' she ain' lay her eyes on P'laski.

She done 'clar' so partic'lar I mos' inclin' to
b'lieve her; but all on a suddent I heah some
'n' sneeze, 'Quechew!' De soun' come f'om
onder de bed, an' I jes retch over an' gether
in my bunch o' hick'ries, an' I say, 'Come
out!' Lucindy say, 'Dat's a cat'; an' I say,
'Yes,' I say, 'hit's a cat I gwine skin, too.'

"I jes stoop down, an' peep onder de bed,
an', sho 'nough, dyah wuz P'laski squinch up
onder dyah, cane an' seegar an' all, jes like a
ole hyah in a trap. I ketch him by de leg, an'
juck him out, an' — don' you know, suh, dat
ooman had done put *my* shut on dat boy, an'
wuz gettin' ready to precipitate him in flight!
I tolt her it wuz p'intedly oudacious for her
an' her son, after he had done stolt ole Mis'
Taine weddin'-ring, to come to my own
house an' rob me jes like I wuz a hen-roos'!"

"What reply did she make to that?" I
asked, to facilitate his narrative.

"She 'ain' possessed no reply to dat indict-
ment," he said, pompously. "She glad by
dat time to remit me to terminate my excitement on P'laski, an' so I did. He hollered
tell dee say you could heah him two miles;
he fyahly lumbered." The old fellow gave a
chuckle of satisfaction at the reminiscence,

and began to draw figures in the sand with his long stick. Suddenly, however, he looked up. "Ef I had a-intimated how much tribilation dat lumberin' wuz gwine to get me in, he nuver would 'a' hollered. Dat come o' dat chicken-stealin' nigger Jem Sinkfiel'; he cyahed him off."

He again became reflective, so I asked, "Haven't you seen him since?"

"Oh, yes, suh, I seen him since," he answered. "I seen him after I come out o' jail; but 'twuz a right close thing. I thought I wuz gone."

"Gone! for whipping him?"

"Nor, suh; 'bout de murder."

"Murder?"

"Yes, suh; murder o' him — o' P'laski."

"But you did not murder him?"

"Nor, suh; an' dat wuz whar de trouble presisted. Ef I had a-murdered him I'd 'a' knowed whar he wuz when dee wanted him; but, as 'twair, when de time arrove, I wair unable to perduce him: and I come mighty nigh forfeitin' my life."

My exclamation of astonishment manifestly pleased him, and he proceeded with increased gravity and carefulness of dictation:

" You see, suh, 'twair dis way." He laid
his stick carefully down, and spreading open
the yellowish palm of one hand, laid the in-
dex finger of the other on it, as if it had been
a map. " When I waked up nex' mornin' an'
called P'laski, he did not rappear. He had
departured; an' so had my shut! Ef 't hadn'
been for de garment, I wouldn' 'a' keered so
much, for I knowed I'd git my han's on him
some time: hawgs mos'ly comes up when de
acorns all gone! an' I know hick'ries ain't
gwine stop growin': but I wuz cawnsiderably
tossified decernin' my garment, an' I gin
Lucindy a little direction 'bout dat. But I
jes went on gittin' my sumac, an' whenever
I come 'cross a right straight hick'ry, I geth-
ered dat too, an' laid it by, 'cus hick'ries grow
mighty fine in ole fiel's whar growin' up like.
An' one day I wuz down in de bushes, an'
Mr. 'Lias Lumpkins, de constable, come ridin' down dyah whar I wuz, an' ax me whar
P'laski is. Hit come in my mind torectly
dat he warn' P'laski 'bout de ring, an' I tell
him I air not aware whar P'laski is: and den
he tell me he got warrant for me, and I mus'
come on wid him. I still reposed, in co'se,
'twuz 'bout de ring, an' I say I ain' had nut-

'tin' to do wid it. An' he say, 'Wid what?'
An' I say, 'Wid de ring.' Den he say,
'Oh!' an' he say, ''Tain' nuttin' 'bout de
ring; 'tis for murder.' Well, I know I ain'
murder nobody, an' I ax him who dee say
I done murder; an' he ax me agin, 'Whar
air P'laski?' I tell him I don' know whar
P'laski air: I know I ain' murder him! Well,
suh, hit subsequently repeared dat dis wuz
de wuss thing I could 'a' said, 'cus when
de trial come on, Major Torm Woods made
mo' o' dat 'n anything else at all; an' hit
'pears like ef you's skused o' murder er steal-
in', you mus'n' say you ain' do it, 'cuz dat's
dangersomer 'n allowing you *is* do it.

"Well, I went 'long wid him. I ax him to
le' me go by my house; but he say, nor, he
'ain' got time, dat he done been dyah. An' he
teck me 'long to de cote-house, an' *lock me up
in de jail!* an' lef' me dyah in de dark on
de rock flo'! An' dyah I rejourned all night
long. An' I might 'a' been dyah now, ef 't
hadn' been dat de co'te come on. Nex' mornin' Mr. Landy Wilde come in dyah an' ax me
how I gettin' on, an' ef I warn' anything. I
tell him I gettin' on toler'ble, an' I ain' warn'
nuttin' but a little tobacco. I warn' git out,

but I knew I cyarn do dat, 'cuz 'twuz de am-
bitiouses smellin' place I ever smelt in my
life. I tell you, suh, I is done smell all de
smells o' mink an' mus' an' puffume, but I
ain' nuver smell nuttin' like dat jail. Mr.
Landy Wilde had to hole he nose while he
in dyah; an' he say he'll git de ole jedge to
come an' ac' as my council. I tell him, 'Nor;
Gord put me in dyah, an' I reckon He'll git
me out when He ready.' I tell you, suh, I
wair p'intedly ashamed for de ole jedge, whar
wuz a gent'man, to come in sich a scand'lous
smellin' place as dat. But de ole jedge come;
an' he say it wuz a —— shame to put a hu-
min in sich place, an' he'd git me bail; which
I mus' say — even ef he is a church member
— might be ixcused ef you jes consider dat
smell. But when de cote meet, dee wouldn'
gi' me no bail, 'cuz dee say I done commit
murder; an' I heah Jim Sinkfiel' an' Mr.
Lumpkins an' ole Mis' Twine went in an'
tole de gran' jury I sutney had murder P'laski,
an' bury him down in de sumac bushes; an'
dee had de gre't bundle o' switches dee fine
in my house, an' dee redite me, an' say ef I
'ain' murder him, why'n't I go 'long an' pre-
duce him. Dat's a curisome thing, suh; dee

tell you to go 'long and fine anybody, an' den
lock you up in jail a insec' couldn' get out."

I agreed with him as to the apparent in-
consistency of this, and he proceeded:

" Well, suh, at las' de trial come on; 'twuz
April cote, an' dee had me in the cote-house,
an' set me down in de cheer, wid de jury right
in front o' me, an' de jedge settin' up in he pul-
pit, lookin' mighty aggrevated. Dat wuz de
fus' time I 'gin to feel maybe I wuz sort o'
forgittin' things, I had done been thinkin' so
much lately in jail 'bout de ole doctor — dat's
ole master — an' Marth' Ann, an' all de ole
times in Hanover, I wuz sort o' misty as I
wuz settin' dyah in de cheer, an' I jes heah
sort o' buzzin' roun' me, an' I warn' altogether certified dat I warn' back in ole Hanover. Den I heah 'em say dat de ole jedge
wuz tooken down an' wuz ixpected to die, an'
dee ax me don' I want a continuance. I don'
know what dat mean, 'sep dee say I have to
go back to jail, an' sense I smell de fresh air I
don' warn' do dat no mo'; so I tell 'em, 'Nor;
I ready to die.' An' den dee made me stan'
up; an' dee read dat long paper to me 'bout
how I done murder P'laski; dee say I had
done whup him to death, an' had done shoot

him, an' knock him in de haid, an' kill him mo' ways 'n 'twould 'a' teck to kill him ef he had been a cat. Lucindy wuz dyah. I had done had her gwine 'bout right smart meckin' quiration for P'laski. At least she *say* she had," he said, with a sudden reservation, and a glance of some suspicion toward his spouse. "An' dee wuz a whole parcel o' niggers stan'-in' roun' dyah, black as buzzards roun' a ole hoss whar dyin'. An' don' you know, dat Jim Sinkfiel' say he sutney hope dee would hang me, an' all jes 'cuz he owe' me two dollars an' seventy-three cents, whar he ain' warn' pay me!"

"Did you not have counsel?" I inquired.

"Council?"

"Yes — a lawyer."

"Oh, nor, suh; dat is, I had council, but not a la'yar, edzactly," he replied, with careful discrimination. "I had a some sort of a la'yer, but not much of a one. I had ixpected ole Jedge Thomas to git me off; 'cuz he knowed me; he wuz a gent'man, like we is; but when he wuz tooken sick so providential I wouldn' had no urrs; I lef' it to Gord. De jedge ax me at de trial didn' I had no la'yar, and I tell him nor, not dyah; an' he ax me

didn' I had no money to get one; an' I er-
spon' ' Nor, I didn' had none,' although I had
at dat time forty-three dollars an' sixty-eight
cents in a ole rag in my waistcoat linin', whar
I had wid me down in de sumac bushes, an'
whar I thought I better hole on to, an' 'ain'
made no mention on. So den de jedge ax me
wouldn' I had a young man dyah — a right
tall young man; an' I enform him: ' Yes,
suh. I didn' reckon 'twould hu't none.' So
den he come an' set by me an' say he wuz my
counsel."

There was such a suggestion of contempt
in his tone that I inquired if he had not done
very well.

"Oh, yes, suh," he drawled, slowly, "he
done toler'ble well — considerin'. He do de
bes' he kin, I reckon. He holler an' mix me
up some right smart; but dee wuz too strong
for him; he warn' no mo' to 'em 'n wurrm is
to woodpecker. Major Torm Woods' de com-
monwealph's attorney, is a powerful la'yer;
he holler so you kin heah him *three* mile.
An' ole Mis' Twine wuz dyah, whar tell all
'bout de ring, an' how impident I wuz to her
dat day, an' skeer her to death. An' dat Jim
Sinkfiel', he wuz dyah, an' tolt' 'bout how I

beat P'laski, an' how he heah him 'way out in
main road, hollerin' 'murder.' An' dee had
de gre't bundle o' hick'ries dyah, whar dee
done fine in my house, an' dee had so much
evidence dat presney I 'mos' begin to think
maybe I had done kilt P'laski sho 'nough, an'
had disermembered it. An' I thought 'bout
Marth' Ann an' all de urr chil'ern, an' I
wondered ef dee wuz to hang me ef I wouldn'
fine her; an' I got so I mos' hoped dee would
sen' me. An den de jury went out, an' stay
some time, an' come back an' say I wuz guilty,
an' sen' me to de Pen'tentiy for six years."

I had followed him so closely, and been so
satisfied of his innocence, that I was surprised
into an exclamation of astonishment, at which
he was evidently much pleased.

"What did your counsel do?" I asked.

He put his head on one side. "He? He
jes lean over an' ax did I warn' to repeal. I
tell him I didn't know. Den he ax me is
I got any money at all. I tell him, nor; ef I
had I would 'a' got me a la'yer."

"What happened then?" I inquired, laughing at his discomfiting reply.

"Well, den de jedge tole me to stan' up,
an' ax me has I got anything to say. Well,

I know dat my las' chance, an' I tell him,
' Yes, suh.' An' he inform me to precede wid
de relation, an' so I did. I preceded, an' I
tolt 'em dyah in de cote-house ev'y wud jes
like I have explanified it heah. I tolt 'em
all 'bout Marth' Ann an' de chillern I hed had;
I reformed 'em all decernin' de Maconses; an'
I notified 'em how P'laski wuz dat urr ooman's
son, not Marth' Ann's, an 'bout de tunament
an' how I had demonstrated wid him not to
ride dyah, an' how he had repudiated my ad-
monition, an' had crown de queen wid ole Mis'
Twine weddin'-ring, whar he come nigh gittin' me shot fur; an' how I had presented him
de hick'ry, an' 'bout how he had departed de
premises while I wuz 'sleep, an' had purloined
my garment, an' how I wuz waitin' for him,
an' getherin' de hick'ry crap an' all. An' dee
wuz all laughin', 'cuz dee know I wuz relatin'
de gospel truth, an' jes den I heah some o' de
niggers back behine call out, ' Hi! heah he
now!' an' I look roun', an', ef you b'lieve
me, suh, dyah wuz P'laski, jes repeared, all
fixed up, wid he cane an' seegar an' all, jes
like I had drawed he resemblance. He had
done been to Wash'n'n, an' had done come
back to see de hangin'.''

The old fellow broke into such a laugh at
the reminiscence that I asked him, " Well,
what was the result?"

" De result, suh, wuz, de jury teck back all
dee had say, an' ax me to go down to de tav-
ern an' have much whiskey as I could stan'
up to, an' dee'd pay for it; an' de jedge dis-
tructed 'em to tu'n me loose. P'laski, he wuz
sort o' bothered; he ain' know wherr to be
disapp'inted 'bout de hangin' or pleased wid
bein' set up so as de centre of distraction, tell
ole Mis' Twine begin to talk 'bout 'restin' of
him. Dat set him back; but I ax 'em, b'fo'
dee 'rest him, couldn' I have jurisdictionment
on him for a leetle while. Dee grant my be-
ques', 'cuz dee know I gwine to erward him
accordin' to his becessities, an' I jes nod
my head to him an' went out. When we got
roun' hine de jail, I invite him to perject his
coat. He nex' garment wuz my own shut,
an' I tolt him to remove dat too; dat I had
to get nigh to he backbone, an' I couldn't
'ford to weah out dat shut no mor'n he had
done already weah it. Somebody had done
fetch de bunch o' hick'ries whar dee had done
fine in my house, an' hit jes like Providence.
I lay 'em by me while I put him on de altar. I

jes made him wrop he arms roun' a little locus'-
tree, an' I fasten he wris'es wid he own gal-
lowses, 'cuz I didn' warn' was'e dem hick'ries;
an' all de time I bindin' him I tellin' him
'bout he sins. Den, when I had him ready, I
begin, an' I rehearse de motter wid him f'om
de time he had ax me 'bout de tunament spang
tell he come to see me hang, an' wid ev'y wud
I gin him de admonish*ment*, tell when I got thoo
wid him he wouldn' 'a' tetch a ring ef he had
been in 'em up to he neck; an' as to shuts, he
would' a' gone naked in frost b'fo' he'd 'a' put
one on. He back gin out b'fo' my hick'ries
did; but I didn' wholly lors 'em. I receive
de valyationo' dem too, 'cuz when I let up on
P'laski, fust man I see wuz dat Jim Sinkfiel',
whar had warn' me hanged 'cuz he didn't warn'
pay me two dollars an' seventy-three cents.
He wuz standin' dyah lookin' on, 'joyin' hiself.
I jes walk up to him an' I tolt him dat he could
pay it right den, or recommodate me to teck
de res' o' de hick'ries. He try to blunder out
o' it, but all de folks know 'bout it an' dee
wuz wid me, an' b'fo' he knowed it some on
'em had he coat off, an' had stretch him
roun' de tree, an' tolt me to perceed. An'
I perceeded.

"I hadn't quite wo' out one hick'ry when he holler dat he'd borry de money an' pay it; but I tolt him, nor; hick'ries had riz; dat I had three mo', an' I warn' show him a man can meck a boy holler 'murder' an' yit not kill him. An' dat I did, too: b'fo' I wuz done he hollered 'murder' jes natchel as P'laski."

The old fellow's countenance beamed with satisfaction at the recollection of his revenge. I rewarded his narrative with a donation which he evidently considered liberal; for he not only was profuse in his thanks, but he assured me that the county of Hanover had produced four people of whom he was duly proud — Henry Clay, Doctor Macon, myself, and himself.

"RUN TO SEED."

Jim's father died at Gettysburg; up against the Stone Fence; went to heaven in a chariot of fire on that fateful day when the issue between the two parts of the country was decided: when the slaughter on the Confederate side was such that after the battle a lieutenant was in charge of a regiment, and a major commanded a brigade.

This fact was much to Jim, though no one knew it: it tempered his mind: ruled his life. He never remembered the time when he did not know the story his mother, in her worn black dress and with her pale face, used to tell him of the bullet-dented sword and faded red sash which hung on the chamber wall.

They were the poorest people in the neighborhood. Everybody was poor; for the county lay in the track of the armies, and the war had swept the country as clean as a floor. But the Uptons were the poorest even in that community. Others recuperated, pulled

147

themselves together, and began after a time to get up. The Uptons got flatter than they were before. The fences (the few that were left) rotted; the fields grew up in sassafras and pines; the barns blew down; the houses decayed; the ditches filled; the chills came.

"They're the shiftlesses' people in the worl'," said Mrs. Wagoner with a shade of asperity in her voice (or was it satisfaction?). Mrs. Wagoner's husband had been in a bomb-proof during the war, when Jim Upton (Jim's father) was with his company. He had managed to keep his teams from the quarter-masters, and had turned up after the war the richest man in the neighborhood. He lived on old Colonel Duval's place, which he had bought for Confederate money.

"They're the shiftlesses' people in the worl'," said Mrs. Wagoner. "Mrs. Upton ain't got any spirit: she jus' sets still and cries her eyes out."

This was true, every word of it. And so was something else that Mrs. Wagoner said in a tone of reprobation, about "people who made their beds having to lay on them"; this process of incubation being too well known to require further discussion.

But what could Mrs. Upton do? She could not change the course of Destiny. One — especially if she is a widow with bad eyes, and in feeble health, living on the poorest place in the State — cannot stop the stars in their courses. She could not blot out the past, nor undo what she had done. She would not if she could. She could not undo what she had done when she ran away with Jim and married him. She would not if she could. At least, the memory of those three years was hers, and nothing could take it from her — not debts, nor courts, nor anything. She knew he was wild when she married him. Certainly Mrs. Wagoner had been careful enough to tell her so, and to tell every one else so too. She would never forget the things she had said. Mrs. Wagoner never forgot the things the young girl said either — though it was more the way she had looked than what she had said. And when Mrs. Wagoner descanted on the poverty of the Uptons she used to end with the declaration: "Well, it ain't any fault of *mine :* she can't blame *me*, for Heaven knows I warned her: I did *my* duty!" Which was true. Warning others was a duty Mrs. Wagoner seldom omitted. Mrs. Upton never thought of blaming her, or any one else. Not all her poverty ever drew one complaint from her sad lips. She simply sat down under it, that was all. She did not expect anything else. She had given her Jim to the South as gladly as any woman ever gave her heart to her love. She would not undo it if she could — not even to have him back, and God knew how much she wanted him. Was not his death glorious — his name a heritage for his son? She could not undo the debts which encumbered the land; nor the interest which swallowed it up; nor the suit which took it from her — that is, all but the old house and the two poor worn old fields which were her dower. She would have given up those too if it had not been for her children, Jim and Kitty, and for the little old enclosure on the hill under the big thorn-trees where they had laid him when they brought him back in the broken pine box from Gettysburg. No, she could not undo the past, nor alter the present, nor change the future. So what could she do?

In her heart Mrs. Wagoner was glad of the poverty of the Uptons; not merely glad in

the general negative way which warms the
bosoms of most of us as we consider how
much better off we are than our neighbors —
the " Lord-I-thank-thee-that-I-am-not-as-other-
men-are " way;—but Mrs. Wagoner was glad
positively. She was glad that any of the
Uptons and the Duvals were poor. One of
her grandfathers had been what Mrs. Wagoner
(when she mentioned the matter at all) called
" Manager " for one of the Duvals. She was
aware that most people did not accept that
term. She remembered old Colonel Duval —
the *old* Colonel — tall, thin, white, grave.
She had been dreadfully afraid of him. She
had had a feeling of satisfaction at his funeral.
It was like the feeling she had when she
learned that Colonel Duval had not forgiven
Betty nor left her a cent.

Mrs. Wagoner used to go to see Mrs. Upton
— she went frequently. It was " her duty "
she said. She carried her things — especially
advice. There are people whose visits are
like spells of illness. It took Mrs. Upton
a fortnight to get over one of these visits —
to convalesce. Mrs. Wagoner was " a mother
to her ": at least, Mrs. Wagoner herself said
so. In some respects it was rather akin to

the substance of that name which forms in vinegar. It was hard to swallow: it galled. Even Mrs. Upton's gentleness was overtaxed — and rebelled. She had stood all the homilies — all the advice. But when Mrs. Wagoner, with her lips drawn in, after wringing her heart, recalled to her the warning she had given her before she married, she stopped standing it. She did not say much; but it was enough to make Mrs. Wagoner's stiff bonnet-bows tremble. Mrs. Wagoner walked out feeling chills down her spine, as if Colonel Duval were at her heels. She had "meant to talk about sending Jim to school": at least she said so. She condoled with every one in the neighborhood on the " wretched ignorance " in which Jim was growing up, " working like a common negro." She called him " that ugly boy."

Jim was ugly — Mrs. Wagoner said, very ugly. He was slim, red-headed, freckle-faced, weak-eyed; he stooped and he stammered. Yet there was something about him, with his thin features, which made one look twice. Mrs. Wagoner used to say she did not know where that boy got all his ugliness from, for she must admit his father was rather good-

looking before he became so bloated, and
Betty Duval would have been " passable " if
she had had any " vivacity." There were
people who said Betty Duval had been a
beauty. She was careful in her limitations,
Mrs. Wagoner was. Some women will not
admit others are pretty, no matter what the
difference in their ages : they feel as if they
were making admissions against themselves.

Once when Jim was a boy Mrs. Wagoner
had the good taste to refer in his presence
to his " homeliness," a term with which she
sugar-coated her insult. Jim grinned and
shuffled his feet, and then said, " Kitty's
pretty." It was true : Kitty was pretty : she
had eyes and hair. You could not look at
her without seeing them — big brown eyes,
and brown tumbled hair. Kitty was fifteen —
two years younger than Jim in 187–.

Jim never went to school. They were too
poor. All he knew his mother taught him
and he got out of the few old books in the
book-case left by the war, — odd volumes of
the Waverley novels, and the *Spectator*, " Don
Quixote," and a few others, stained and bat-
tered. He could not have gone to school if
there had been a school to go to : he had to

work: work, as Mrs. Wagoner had truthfully said, "like a common nigger." He did not mind it; a bird born in a cage cannot mind it much. The pitiful part is, it does not know anything else. Jim did not know anything else. He did not mind anything much — except chills. He even got used to them; would just lie down and shake for an hour and then go to ploughing again as soon as the ague was over, with the fever on him. He had to plough; for corn was necessary. He had this compensation: he was worshipped by two people — his mother and Kitty. If other people thought him ugly, they thought him beautiful. If others thought him dull, they thought him wonderfully clever; if others thought him ignorant, they knew how wise he was.

Mrs. Upton's eyes were bad; but she saw enough to see Jim: the light came into the house with him; Kitty sat and gazed at him with speechless admiration; hung on his words, which were few; watched for his smile, which was rare. He repaid it to her by being — Jim. He slaved for her; waited for her (when a boy waits for his little sister it is something); played with her when he had

time (this also was something); made traps
for her; caught her young squirrels, — was at
once her slave and her idol. As he grew up
he did not have time to play. He had to
plough: "just like a common nigger," Mrs.
Wagoner said with an unclouded face. In
this she spoke the truth.

It is a curious thing that farming paid better shortly after the war than it did later.
Lands fell. Times grew harder. They were
always growing harder with Jim. The land
was worked out. Guano was necessary to
make anything grow. Guano was bought on
credit. The crops would not pay. Several
summers there was drouth; crops failed.
One of the two old mules that he had died;
Jim ploughed with one. Then he broke his
leg. When he got about again he was lame:
the leg had shortened.

"They're the shiftlesses' folks in the worl',"
said Mrs. Wagoner; "they can't blame *me*.
Heaven knows I told ——" etc. Which was
true — more than true.

Jim ploughed on, only slower than ever,
thinner than ever, sleepier than ever.

One day something happened which waked
him up. It was a Sunday. They went to

church; they always went to church—old St.
Ann's — whenever there was service. There
was service there since the war only every
first and third Sunday and every other fifth
Sunday. The Uptons and the Duvals had
been vestrymen from the time they had
brought the bricks over from England, generations ago. They had sat, one family in
one of the front semicircular pews on one
side the chancel, the other family in the
other. Mrs. Upton, after the war, had her
choice of the pews; for all had gone but herself, Jim, and Kitty. She had changed, the
Sunday after her marriage, to the Upton side,
and she clung loyally to it ever after. Mrs.
Wagoner had taken the other pew — a cold,
she explained at first, had made her deaf.
She always spoke of it afterward as "our
pew." (The Billings, from which Mrs.
Wagoner came, had not been Episcopalians
until Mrs. Wagoner married.) Carry Wagoner, who was a year older than Kitty, used
to sit by her mother, with her big hat and
brown hair. Jim, in right of his sex, sat
in the end of his pew.

On this Sunday in question Jim drove his
mother and Kitty to church in the horse cart.

The old carriage was a wreck, slowly dropping to pieces. The chickens roosted in it.
The cart was the only vehicle remaining
which had two sound wheels, and even one
of these "wabbled" a good deal, and the
cart was "shackling." But straw placed
in the bottom made it fairly comfortable.
Jim always had clean straw in it for his
mother and sister. His mother and Kitty re-
marked on it. Kitty looked so well. They
reached church. The day was warm, Mr.
Bickersteth was dry. Jim went to sleep during the sermon. He frequently did this. He
had been up since four. When service was
over he partially waked — about half-waked.
He was standing in the aisle moving toward
the door with the rest of the congregation. A
voice behind him caught his ear:

"What a lovely girl Kitty Upton is." It
was Mrs. Harrison, who lived at the other end
of the parish. Jim knew the voice. Another
voice replied:

"If she only were not always so *shabby!*"
Jim knew this voice also. It was Mrs. Wagoner's. Jim waked.

"Yes, but even her old darned dress cannot hide her. She reminds me of ——" Jim

did not know what it was to which Mrs. Harrison likened her. But he knew it was something beautiful.

"Yes," said Mrs. Wagoner; then added, "Poor thing, she's got no education, and never will have. To think that old Colonel Duval's fam'bly's come to this! Well, they can't blame me. They're clean run to seed."

Jim got out into the air. He felt sick. He had been hit vitally. This was what people thought! and it was true. They were "clean run to seed." He went to get his cart. (He did not speak to Kitty.) His home came before his eyes like a photograph: fences down, gates gone, houses ruinous, fields barren. It came to him as if stamped on the retina by a lightning-flash. He had worked — worked hard. But it was no use. It was true: they were "clean run to seed." He helped his mother and Kitty into the cart silently — doggedly. Kitty smiled at him. It hurt him like a blow. He saw every worn place, every darn in her old dress, and little, faded jacket. Mrs. Wagoner drove past them in her carriage, leaning out of the window and calling that she took the liberty of passing as she drove faster than they. Jim gave his old mule a jerk which made him throw up his head and wince with pain. He was sorry for it. But he had been jerked up short himself. He was quivering too.

II.

On the following Friday the President of one of the great railway lines which cross Virginia was in his office when the door opened after a gentle knock and some one entered. (The offices of presidents of railroads had not then become the secret and mysterious sanctums which they have since become.) The President was busily engaged with two or three of the Directors, wealthy capitalists from the North, who had come down on important business. He was very much engrossed; and he did not look up immediately. When he did so he saw standing inside the door a queer figure, — long, slim, angular, — a man who looked like a boy, or a boy who looked like a man — red-headed, freckled-faced, bashful, — in a coat too tight even for his thin figure, breeches too short for his long legs; his hat was old and brown; his shirt was clean.

" Well, what do you want?" The President was busy.

It was Jim. His face twitched several times before any sound came:

" – – I- w- w- w want t- t- t- to ge- get a place."

" This is not the place to get it. I have no place for you."

The President turned back to his friends. At the end of ten minutes, seeing one of his visitors look toward the door, he stopped in the middle of a sentence and glanced around.

The figure was still there — motionless. The President thought he had been out and come back. He had not.

" Well?" His key was high.

" – – – – I- I- w- w- want to- to get a place."

" I told you I had no place for you. Go to the Superintendent."

" – – – I- I've b- b- b- been to him."

" Well, what did he say?"

" S- s- s- says he ain't got any place."

" Well, I haven't any. Go to Mr. Blake."

" – – – Iv'e b- been to *him*."

" Well, go to — to — " The President was looking for a paper. It occupied his mind.

He did not think any further of Jim. But Jim was there.

"– – Go– go where ? "

"Oh, I don't know — go anywhere — go out of *here.*"

Jim's face worked. He turned and went slowly out. As he reached the door he said:

" Go– go– good-evening g– gentlemen."

The President's heart relented: "Go to the Superintendent," he called.

Next day he was engaged with his Directors when the door opened and the same apparition stepped within — tall, slim, red-haired, with his little tight coat, short trousers, and clean shirt.

The President frowned.

" Well, what is it ? "

"– – – I– I– I w– w– w– went to– to the S– S– Superintendent."

" Well, what about it ? "

" Y– y– you told me to– to go– go to him. H– e– e ain't got any place." The Directors smiled. One of them leaned back in his chair, took out a cigar and prepared to cut the end.

" Well, I can't help it. I haven't anything for you. I told you that yesterday. You must not come here bothering me; get out."

Jim stood perfectly still — perfectly motionless. He looked as if he had been there always — would be there always. The Director with the cigar, having cut it, took out a gold match-box, and opened it slowly, looking at Jim with an amused smile. The President frowned and opened his mouth to order him out. He changed his mind.

" What is your name ? "

" J— J— James Upton."

" Where from ? "

Jim told him.

" Whose son are you ? "

" C— C— C— Captain J— J— James Upton's."

" What! You don't look much like him!"

Jim shuffled one foot. One corner of his mouth twitched up curiously. It might have been a smile. He looked straight at the blank wall before him.

" You are not much like your mother either — I used to know her as a girl. How's that ? "

Jim shuffled the other foot a little.

" R— r— run to seed, I reckon."

The President was a farmer — prided himself on it. The reply pleased him. He touched a bell. A clerk entered.

"Ask Mr. Wake to come here."

"Can you carry a barrel of flour?" he asked Jim.

" I– I'll get it there," said Jim.   He leaned a little forward.   His eyes opened.

" Or a sack of salt ?   They are right heavy."

" I– I– I'll get it there," said Jim.   His form straightened.

Mr. Wake appeared.

" Write Mr. Day to give this man a place as brakeman."

" Yes, sir.   Come this way."   This to Jim.

Jim electrified them all by suddenly bursting out crying.

The tension had given way.   He walked up to the wall and leaned his head against it with his face on his arm, shaking from head to foot, sobbing aloud.

" Thank you, I — I'm ever so much obliged to you," he sobbed.

The President rose and walked rapidly about the room.

Suddenly Jim turned and, with his arm over his eyes, held out his hand to the President.

" Good-by."   Then he went out.

There was a curious smile on the faces of the Directors as the door closed.

"Well, I never saw anything like that before," said one of them. The President said nothing.

"Run to seed," quoted the oldest of the Directors, "rather good expression!"

"Damned good seed, gentlemen," said the President, a little shortly. "Duval and Upton. — That fellow's father was in my command. Died at Gettysburg. He'd fight hell."

Jim got a place — brakeman on a freight-train.

That night Jim wrote a letter home. You'd have thought he had been elected President.

It was a hard life: harder than most. The work was hard; the fare was hard; the life was hard. Standing on top of rattling cars as they rushed along in the night around curves, over bridges, through tunnels, with the rain and snow pelting in your face, and the tops as slippery as ice. There was excitement about it, too: a sense of risk and danger. Jim did not mind it much. He thought of his mother and Kitty.

There was a freemasonry among the men. All knew each other; hated or liked each other; nothing negative about it.

It was a bad road. Worse than the average. Twice the amount of traffic was done on the single track that should have been done. Result was men were ground up — more than on most roads. More men were killed in proportion to the number employed than were killed in service during the war. The *esprit de corps* was strong. Men stood by their trains and by each other. When a man left his engine in sight of trouble, the authorities might not know about it, but the men did. Unless there was cause he had to leave. Sam Wray left his engine in sight of a broken bridge after he reversed. The engine stopped on the track. The officers never knew of it; but Wray and his fireman both changed to another road. When a man even got shaky and began to run easy, the superintendent might not mind it; but the men did: he had to go. A man had to have not only courage but nerve.

Jim was not especially popular among men. He was reserved, slow, awkward. He was "pious" (that is, did not swear). He was "stuck up" (did not tell "funny things," by which was meant vulgar stories; nor laugh at them either). And according to Dick Rail, he was "stingy as h—l."

These things were not calculated to make
him popular, and he was not. He was a sort
of butt for the free and easy men who lived
in their cabs and cabooses, obeyed their "orders," and owned nothing but their overalls
and their shiny Sunday clothes. He was
good-tempered, though. Took all their gibes
and "dev'ling" quietly, and for the most part
silently. So, few actually disliked him. Dick
Rail, the engineer of his crew, was one of
those few. Dick "dee-spised" him. Dick was
big, brawny, coarse : coarse in looks, coarse
in talk, coarse every way, and when he had
liquor in him he was mean. Jim "bothered"
him, he said. He made Jim's life a burden
to him. He laid himself out to do it. It
became his occupation. He thought about it
when Jim was not present; laid plans for it.
There was something about Jim that was different from most others. When Jim did not
laugh at a "hard story," but just sat still,
some men would stop; Dick always told another harder yet, and called attention to Jim's
looks. His stock was inexhaustible. His
mind was like a spring which ran muddy
water; its flow was perpetual. The men
thought Jim did not mind. He lost three

pounds; which for a man who was six feet
(and would have been six feet two if he had
been straight) and who weighed 122, was
considerable.

It is astonishing how one man can create
a public sentiment. One woman can ruin a
reputation as effectually as a churchful. One
bullet can kill a man as dead as a bushel, if
it hits him right. So Dick Rail injured Jim.
For Dick was an authority. He swore the
biggest oaths, wore the largest watch-chain,
knew his engine better and sat it steadier
than any man on the road. He had had a
passenger train again and again, but he was
too fond of whiskey. It was too risky. Dick
affected Jim's standing: told stories about
him: made his life a burden to him. " He
shan't stay on the road," he used to say.
" He's stingier'n ——! Carries his victuals
about with him — I b'lieve he sleeps with one
o' them *I*-talians in a goods box." This was
true — at least, about carrying his food with
him. (The rest was Dick's humor.) Mess-
ing cost too much. The first two months'
pay went to settle an old guano-bill; but the
third month's pay was Jim's. The day he
drew that he fattened a good deal. At least,

he looked so. It was eighty-two dollars (for Jim ran extra runs;—made double time whenever he could). Jim had never had so much money in his life; had hardly ever seen it. He walked about the streets that night till nearly midnight, feeling the wad of notes in his breast-pocket. Next day a box went down the country, and a letter with it, and that night Jim could not have bought a chew of tobacco. The next letter he got from home was heavy. Jim smiled over it a good deal, and cried a little too. He wondered how Kitty looked in her new dress, and if the barrel of flour made good bread; and if his mother's shawl was warm.

One day he was changed to the passenger service, the express. It was a promotion, paid more, and relieved him from Dick Rail.

He had some queer experiences being ordered around, but he swallowed them all. He had not been there three weeks when Mrs. Wagoner was a passenger on the train. Carry was with her. They had moved to town. (Mr. Wagoner was interested in railroad development.) Mrs. Wagoner called him to her seat, and talked to him—in a loud voice. Mrs. Wagoner had a loud voice.

It had the "carrying" quality. She did not shake hands; Carry did and said she was so glad to see him: she had been down home the week before — had seen his mother and Kitty. Mrs. Wagoner said, "We still keep our plantation as a country place." Carry said Kitty looked so well; her new dress was lovely. Mrs. Wagoner said his mother's eyes were worse. She and Kitty had walked over to see them, to show Kitty's new dress. She had promised that Mr. Wagoner would do what he could for him (Jim) on the road.

Next month Jim went back to the freight service. He preferred Dick Rail to Mrs. Wagoner. He got him. Dick was worse than ever, his appetite was whetted by abstinence; he returned to his attack with renewed zest. He never tired — never flagged. He was perpetual: he was remorseless. He made Jim's life a wilderness. Jim said nothing, just slouched along silenter than ever, quieter than ever, closer than ever. He took to going on Sunday to another church than the one he had attended, a more fashionable one than that. The Wagoners went there. Jim sat far back in the gallery, very far back, where he could just see the top of

Carry's head, her big hat and her face, and could not see Mrs. Wagoner, who sat nearer the gallery. It had a curious effect on him: he never went to sleep there. He took to going up-town walking by the stores — looking in at the windows of tailors and clothiers. Once he actually went into a shop and asked the price of a new suit of clothes. (He needed them badly.) The tailor unfolded many rolls of cloth and talked volubly: talked him dizzy. Jim looked wistfully at them, rubbed his hand over them softly, felt the money in his pocket; and came out. He said he thought he might come in again. Next day he did not have the money. Kitty wrote him she could not leave home to go to school on their mother's account, but she would buy books, and she was learning; she would learn fast, her mother was teaching her; and he was the best brother in the world, the whole world; and they had a secret, but he must wait.

One day Jim got a big bundle from down the country. It was a new suit of clothes. On top was a letter from Kitty. This was the secret. She and her mother had sent for the cloth and had made them; they

hoped they would fit. They had cried over
them. Jim cried a little too. He put them
on. They did not fit, were much too large.
Under Dick Rail's fire Jim had grown even
thinner than before. But he wore them
to church. He felt that it would have been
untrue to his mother and Kitty not to wear
them. He was sorry to meet Dick Rail on
the street. Dick had on a black broadcloth
coat, a velvet vest, and large-checked trousers. Dick looked Jim over. Jim winced,
flushed a little : he was not so sunburned now.
Dick saw it. Next week Dick caught Jim
in a crowd in the "yard" waiting for their
train. He told about the meeting. He made a
double shot. He said, " Boys, Jim's in love,
he's got new clothes ! you ought to see 'em !"
Dick was graphic; he wound up: " They
hung on him like breechin' on his old mule.
By ——! I b'lieve he was too —— stingy
to buy 'em and made 'em himself." There
was a shout from the crowd. Jim's face
worked. He jumped for him. There was a
handspike lying near and he seized it. Some
one grabbed him, but he shook him off as if
he had been a child. Why he did not kill
Dick no one ever knew. He meant to do it.

For some time they thought he was dead.
He laid off for over a month.   After that
Jim wore what clothes he chose: no one
ever troubled him.

So he went on in the same way: slow, sleepy,
stuttering, thin, stingy, ill-dressed, lame.

He was made a fireman; preferred it to being a conductor, it led to being an engineer,
which paid more.   He ran extra trips whenever he could, up and double straight back.
He could stand an immense amount of work.
If he got sleepy he put tobacco in his eyes to
keep them open.   It was bad for the eyes,
but waked him up.   Kitty was going to take
music next year, and that cost money.   He
had not been home for several months, but
was going at Christmas.

They did not have any sight tests then.
But the new Directory meant to be thorough.
Mr. Wagoner had become a Director, had his
eye on the presidency.   Jim was one day sent
for, and was asked about his eyes.   They were
bad.   There was not a doubt about it.   They
were inflamed; he could not see a hundred
yards.   He did not tell them about the extra
trips and putting the tobacco in them.   Dick
Rail must have told about him.   They said he

must go. Jim turned white. He went to his little room, close up under the roof of a little dingy house in a back street, and sat down in the dark; thought about his mother and Kitty, and dimly about some one else; wrote his mother and Kitty a letter; said he was coming home — called it "a visit"; cried over the letter, but was careful not to cry on it. He was a real cry-baby — Jim was.

"Just run to seed," he said to himself, bitterly, over and over; "just run to seed." Then he went to sleep.

The following day he went down to the railroad. That was the last day. Next day he would be "off." The train-master saw him and called him. A special was just going out. The Directors were going over the road in the officers' car. Dick Rail was the engineer, and his fireman had been taken sick. Jim must take the place. Jim had a mind not to do it. He hated Dick. He thought of how he had pursued him. But he heard a voice behind him and turned. Carry was standing down the platform, talking with some elderly gentlemen. She had on a travelling cap and ulster. She saw him and came forward — a step:

"How do you do?" she held out her little gloved hand. She was going out over the road with her father. Jim took off his hat and shook hands with her. Dick Rail saw him, walked round the other side of the engine, and tried to take off his hat like that. It was not a success; Dick knew it.

Jim went.

"Who was that?" one of the elderly gentlemen asked Carry.

"An old friend of mine — a gentleman," she said.

"Rather run to seed — hey?" the old fellow quoted, without knowing exactly why; for he only half recognized Jim, if he recognized him at all.

They started.

It was a bad trip. The weather was bad, the road was bad, the engine bad; Dick bad; — worse than all. Jim had a bad time: he was to be off when he got home. What would his mother and Kitty do?

Once Carry came (brought by the President) and rode in the engine for a little while. Jim helped her up and spread his coat for her to sit on, put his overcoat under her feet; his heart was in it. Dick was sul-

len, and Jim had to show her about the engine. When she got down to go back to the
car she thanked him — she " had enjoyed it
greatly " — she " would like to try it again."
Jim smiled. He was almost good-looking
when he smiled.

Dick was meaner than ever after that,
sneered at Jim — swore ; but Jim didn't mind
it. He was thinking of some one else, and of
the rain which would prevent her coming
again.

They were on the return trip, and were
half-way home when the accident happened.
It was just " good dusk," and it had been raining all night and all day, and the road was as
rotten as mud. The special was behind and
was making up. She had the right of way,
and she was flying. She rounded a curve
just above a small " fill," under which was a
little stream, nothing but a mere " branch."
In good weather it would never be noticed.
The gay party behind were at dinner. The first
thing they knew was the sudden jerk which
came from reversing the engine at full speed,
and the grind as the wheels slid along under
the brakes. Then they stopped with a bump
which jerked them out of their seats, set the

lamps to swinging, and sent the things on the
table crashing on the floor. No one was hurt,
only shaken, and they crowded out of the car
to learn the cause. They found it. The engine was half buried in wet earth on the other
side of the little washout, with the tender
jammed up into the cab. The whole was
wrapped in a dense cloud of escaping steam.
The roar was terrific. The big engineer,
bare-headed and covered with mud, and with
his face deadly white, was trying to get
down to the engine. Some one was in
there.

They got him out after a while (but it took
some time), and laid him on the ground, while
a mattress was got. It was Jim.

Carry had been weeping and praying. She
sat down and took his head in her lap, and
with her lace handkerchief wiped his blackened and bleeding face, and smoothed his
wet hair.

The newspaper accounts, which are always
reflections of what public sentiment is, or
should be, spoke of it — some, as "a providential" — others, as "a miraculous" — and yet
others as "a fortunate" escape on the part

of the President and the Directors of the road, according to the tendencies, religious or otherwise, of their paragraphists.

They mentioned casually that "only one person was hurt — an employee, name not ascertained." And one or two had some gush about the devotion of the beautiful young lady, the daughter of one of the directors of the road, who happened to be on the train, and who, "like a ministering angel, held the head of the wounded man in her lap after he was taken from the wreck." A good deal was made of this picture, which was extensively copied.

Dick Rail's account, after he had come back from carrying the broken body down to the old Upton place in the country, and helping to lay it away in the old enclosure under the big trees on the hill, was this :

"By ——! " he said, when he stood in the yard, with a solemn-faced group around him, "we were late, and I was just shaking 'em up. I had been meaner'n hell to Jim all the trip (I didn't know him, and you all didn't neither), and I was workin' him for all he was worth: I didn't give him a minute. The sweat was rolling off him, and I was damnin' him with every shovelful. We was runnin' under orders to make up, and we was just rounding the curve this side of Ridge Hill, when Jim hollered. He saw it as he raised up with the shovel in his hand to wipe the sweat off his face, and he hollered to me, 'My God! Look, Dick! Jump!'

"I looked and Hell was right there. He caught the lever and reversed, and put on the air and sand before I saw it, and then grabbed me, and flung me clean out of the cab: 'Jump!' he says, as he give me a swing. I jumped, expectin' of course he was comin' too; and as I lit, I saw him turn and catch the lever. The old engine was jumpin' nigh off the track. But she was too near. In she went, and the tender right on her. You may talk about his eyes bein' bad; but by ——! when he gave me that swing, they looked to me like coals of fire. When we got him out 'twarn't Jim! He warn't nothin' but mud and ashes. He warn't quite dead; opened his eyes, and breathed onct or twict; but I don't think he knew anything, he was so mashed up. We laid him out on the grass, and that young lady took his head in her lap and cried over him (she had come and seed

him in the engine), and said she knew his
mother and sister down in the country (she
used to live down there) ; they was gentle-
folks; that Jim was all they had. And when
one of them old director-fellows who had been
swilling himself behind there come aroun',
with his kid gloves on and his hands in his
great-coat pockets, lookin' down, and sayin'
something about, ' Poor fellow, couldn't he
'a jumped? Why didn't he jump? ' I let him
have it; I said, ' Yes, and if it hadn't been for
him, you and I'd both been frizzin' in h—l
this minute.' And the President standin'
there said to some of them, ' That was the
same young fellow who came into my office
to get a place last year when you were down,
and said he had "run to seed." ' But,' he
says, 'Gentlemen, it was d——d good seed!'"

How good it was no one knew but two
weeping women in a lonely house.

"A SOLDIER OF THE EMPIRE."

IT was his greatest pride in life that he had been a soldier — a soldier of the empire. He was known simply as " The Soldier," and it is probable that there was not a man or woman, and certain that there was not a child in the Quarter who did not know him: the tall, erect old Sergeant with his white, carefully waxed moustache, and his face seamed with two sabre cuts. One of these cuts, all knew, had been received the summer day when he had stood, a mere boy, in the hollow square at Waterloo, striving to stay the fierce flood of the "men on the white horses"; the other, tradition said, was of even more ancient date.

Yes, they all knew him, and knew how when he was not over thirteen, just the age of little Raoul the humpback, who was not as tall as Pauline, he had received the cross which he always wore over his heart sewed in the breast of his coat, from the hand of

the emperor himself, for standing on the hill
at Wagram when his regiment broke, and
beating the long-roll, whilst he held the
tattered colors resting in his arm, until the
men rallied and swept back the left wing of
the enemy. This the children knew, as their
fathers and mothers and grandfathers and
grandmothers before them had known it, and
rarely an evening passed that some of the
gamins were not to be found in the old man's
kitchen, which was also his parlor, or else
on his little porch, listening with ever-new
delight to the story of his battles and of the
emperor. They all knew as well as he the
thrilling part where the emperor dashed by
(the old Sergeant always rose reverently at
the name, and the little audience also stood,
—one or two nervous younger ones sometimes bobbing up a little ahead of time, but
sitting down again in confusion under the
contemptuous scowls and pluckings of the
rest), —where the emperor dashed by, and
reined up to ask an officer what regiment
that was that had broken, and who was that
drummer that had been promoted to ensign ;
—they all knew how, on the grand review
afterwards, the Sergeant, beating his drum

with one hand (while the other, which had been broken by a bullet, was in a sling), had marched with his company before the emperor, and had been recognized by him. They knew how he had been called up by a staff-officer (whom the children imagined to be a fine gentleman with a rich uniform, and a great shako like Marie's uncle, the drum-major), and how the emperor had taken from his own breast and with his own hand had given him the cross, which he had never from that day removed from his heart, and had said, "I would make you a colonel if I could spare you."

This was the story they liked best, though there were many others which they frequently begged to be told — of march and siege and battle, of victories over or escapes from red-coated Britishers and fierce German lancers, and of how the mere presence of the emperor was worth fifty thousand men, and how the soldiers knew that where he was no enemy could withstand them. It all seemed to them very long ago, and the soldier of the empire was the only man in the Quarter who was felt to be greater than the rich nobles and fine officers who flashed along the great

streets, or glittered through the boulevards
and parks outside. More than once when
Paris was stirred up, and the Quarter seemed
on the eve of an outbreak, a mounted or-
derly had galloped up to his door with a
letter, requesting his presence somewhere (it
was whispered at the prefect's), and when
he returned, if he refused to speak of his
visit the Quarter was satisfied; it trusted
him and knew that when he advised quiet it
was for its good. He loved France first, the
Quarter next. Had he not been offered — ?
What had he not been offered! The Quarter
knew, or fancied it knew, which did quite as
well. At least, it knew how he always took
sides with the Quarter against oppression.
It knew how he had gone up into the burning
tenement and brought the children down out
of the garret just before the roof fell. It
knew how he had jumped into the river that
winter when it was full of ice, to save Raoul's
little lame dog which had fallen into the
water; it knew how he had reported the gendarmes for arresting poor little Aimée just
for begging a man in the Place de L'Opéra
for a franc for her old grandmother, who was
blind, and how he had her released instead

of being sent to ———. But what was the need of multiplying instances! He was " the Sergeant," a soldier of the empire, and there was not a dog in the Quarter which did not feel and look proud when it could trot on the inside of the sidewalk by him.

Thus the old Sergeant came to be regarded as the conservator of order in the Quarter, and was worth more in the way of keeping it quiet than all the gendarmes that ever came inside its precincts. And thus the children all knew him.

One story that the Sergeant sometimes told, the girls liked to hear, though the boys did not, because it had nothing about war in it, and Minette and Clarisse used to cry so when it was told, that the Sergeant would stop and put his arms around them and pet them until they only sobbed on his shoulder.

It was of how he had, when a lonely old man, met down in Lorraine his little Camille, whose eyes were as blue as the sky, and her hand as white as the flower from which she took her name, and her cheeks as pink as the roses in the gardens of the Tuileries. He had loved her, and she, though forty years his junior, had married him and had come

here to live with him; but the close walls of
the city had not suited her, and she had pined
and languished before his eyes like a plucked
lily, and, after she bore him Pierre, had died
in his arms, and left him lonelier than before.
And the old soldier always lowered his voice
and paused a moment (Raoul said he was
saying a mass), and then he would add con-
solingly: "But she left a soldier, and when
I am gone, should France ever need one,
Pierre will be here." The boys did not
fancy this story for the reasons given, and besides, although they loved the Sergeant, they
did not like Pierre. Pierre was not popular
in the Quarter,—except with the young girls
and a few special friends. The women said
he was idle and vain like his mother, who had
been, they said, a silly lazy thing with little
to boast of but blue eyes and a white skin,
of which she was too proud to endanger it
by work, and that she had married the Sergeant for his pension, and would have ruined
him if she had lived, and that Pierre was just
like her.

The children knew nothing of the resemblance. They disliked Pierre because he
was cross and disagreeable to them, and how-

ever their older sisters might admire his curl-
ing brown hair, his dark eyes, and delicate features, which he had likewise inherited from
his mother, they did not like him; for he always scolded when he came home and found
them there; and he had several times ordered
the whole lot out of the house; and once
he had slapped little Raoul, for which Jean
Maison had beaten him. Of late, too, when
it drew near the hour for him to come home,
the old Sergeant had two or three times left
out a part of his story, and had told them to
run away and come back in the morning, as
Pierre liked to be quiet when he came from
his work — which Raoul said was gambling.

Thus it was that Pierre was not popular in
the Quarter.

He was nineteen years old when war was
declared.

They said Prussia was trying to rob France,
— to steal Alsace and Lorraine. All Paris
was in an uproar. The Quarter, always ripe
for any excitement, shared in and enjoyed
the general commotion. It struck off from
work. It was like the commune; at least, so
people said. Pierre was the loudest declaimer
in the district. He got work in the armory.

Recruiting officers went in and out of the
saloons and cafés, drinking with the men,
talking to the women, and stirring up as
much fervor as possible. It needed little to
stir it. The Quarter was seething. Troops
were being mustered in, and the streets and
parks were filled with the tramp of regiments;
and the roll of the drums, the call of the bugles,
and the cheers of the crowds as they marched
by floated into the Quarter. Brass bands
were so common that although in the winter
a couple of strolling musicians had been sufficient to lose temporarily every child in the
Quarter, it now required a full band and a
grenadier regiment, to boot, to draw a toler-
able representation.

Of all the residents of the Quarter, none
took a deeper interest than the soldier of
the empire. He became at once an object
of more than usual attention. He had married in Lorraine, and could, of course, tell just
how long it would take to whip the Prussians.
He thought a single battle would decide it.
It would if the emperor were there. His
little court was always full of inquirers, and
the stories of the emperor were told *to* audi-
ences now of grandfathers and grandmothers.

Once or twice the gendarmes had sauntered down, thinking, from seeing the crowd, that a fight was going on. They had stayed to hear of the emperor. A hint was dropped by the soldier of the empire that perhaps France would conquer Prussia, and then go on across to Moscow to settle an old score, and that night it was circulated through the Quarter that the invasion of Russia would follow the capture of Berlin. The emperor became more popular than he had been since the *coup d'état.* Half the Quarter offered its services.

The troops were being drilled night and day, and morning after morning the soldier of the empire locked his door, buttoned his coat tightly around him, and with a stately military air marched over to the park to see the drill, where he remained until it was time for Pierre to have his supper.

The old Sergeant's acquaintance extended far beyond the Quarter. Indeed, his name had been mentioned in the papers more than once, and his presence was noted at the drill by those high in authority; so that he was often to be seen surrounded by a group listening to his accounts of the emperor, or showing what the *manuel* had been in his time. His air, always soldierly, was now imposing, and many a visitor of distinction inquiring who he might be, and learning that he was a soldier of the empire, sought an introduction to him. Sometimes they told him that they could hardly believe him so old, could hardly believe him much older than some of those in the ranks, and although at first he used to declare he was like a rusty flint-lock, too old and useless for service, their flattery soothed his vanity, and after a while, instead of shaking his head and replying as he did at first that France had no use for old men, he would smile doubtfully and say that when they let Pierre go, maybe he would go too, "just to show the children how they fought then."

The summer came. The war began in earnest. The troops were sent to the front, the crowds shouting, "On to Berlin." Others were mustered in and sent after them as fast as they were equipped. News of battle after battle came; at first, of victory (so the papers said), full and satisfying, then meagre and uncertain, and at last so scanty that only the wise ones knew there had been a defeat. The Quarter was in a fever of patriotism.

Jean Maison and nearly all the young men had enlisted and gone, leaving their sweethearts by turns waving their kerchiefs and wiping their eyes with them. Pierre, however, still remained behind. He said he was working for the Government. Raoul said he was not working at all; that he was skulking.

Suddenly the levy came. Pierre was conscripted.

That night the Sergeant enlisted in the same company. Before the week was out, their regiment was equipped and dispatched to the front, for the news came that the army was making no advance, and it was said that France needed more men. Some shook their heads and said that was not what she needed, that what she needed was better officers. A suggestion of this by some of the recruits in the old Sergeant's presence drew from him the rebuke that in his day "such a speech would have called out a corporal and a file of grenadiers."

The day they were mustered in, the captain of the company sent for him and bade him have the first sergeant's chevrons sewed on his sleeve. The order had come from the colonel, some even said from the marshal. In the Quarter it was said that it came from the emperor. The Sergeant suggested that Pierre was the man for the place; but the captain simply repeated the order. The Quarter approved the selection, and several fights occurred among the children who had gotten up a company as to who should be the sergeant. It was deemed more honorable than to be the captain.

The day the regiment left Paris, the Sergeant was ordered to report several reliable men for special duty; he detailed Pierre among the number. Pierre was sick, so sick that when the company started he would have been left behind but for his father. The old soldier was too proud of his son to allow him to miss the opportunity of fighting for France. Pierre was the handsomest man in the regiment.

The new levies on arrival in the field went into camp, in and near some villages and were drilled, — quite needlessly, Pierre and some of the others declared. They were not accustomed to restraint, and they could not see why they should be worked to death when they were lying in camp doing nothing. But the soldier of the empire was a strict drillmaster, and the company was shortly the best-drilled one in the regiment.

Yet the army lay still: they were not marching on to Berlin. The sole principle of the campaign seemed to be the massing together of as many troops as possible. What they were to do no one appeared very clearly to know. What they were doing all knew: they were doing nothing. The men, at first burning for battle, became cold or lukewarm with waiting; dissatisfaction crept in, and then murmurs: "Why did they not fight?" The soldier of the empire himself was sorely puzzled. The art of war had clearly changed since his day. The emperor would have picked the best third of these troops and have been at the gates of the Prussian capital in less time than they had spent camped with the enemy right before them. Still, it was not for a soldier to question, and he reported for a week's extra guard duty a man who ventured to complain in his presence that the marshal knew as little as the men. Extra guard duty did no good. The army was losing heart.

Thus it was for several weeks. But at last, one evening, it was apparent that some

change was at hand: the army stirred and
shook itself as a great animal moves and
stretches, not knowing if it will awake or
drop off to sleep again.

During the night it became wide awake.
It was high time. The Prussians were almost
on them. They had them in a trap. They
held the higher grounds and hemmed the
French in. All night long the tents were
being struck, and the army was in commotion. No one knew just why it was. Some
said they were about to be attacked; some
said they were surrounded. Uncertainty gave
place to excitement. At length they marched.

When day began to break, the army had
been tumbled into line of battle, and the regiment in which the old Sergeant and Pierre
were was drawn up on the edge of a gentleman's park outside of the villages. The
line extended beyond them farther than they
could see, and large bodies of troops were
massed behind them, and were marching and
countermarching in clouds of dust. The rumor
went along the ranks that they were in the advanced line, and that the Germans were just the
other side of the little plateau, which they could
dimly see in the gray light of the dawn. The

men, having been marching in the dark, were tired, and most of them lay down, when they were halted, to rest. Some went to sleep; others, like Pierre, set to work and with their bayonets dug little trenches and threw up a slight earthwork before them, behind which they could lie; for the skirmishers had been thrown out, looking vague and ghostly as they trotted forward in the dim twilight, and they supposed that the battle would be fought right there. By the time, however, that the trenches were dug, the line was advanced, and the regiment was moved forward some distance, and was halted just under a knoll along which ran a road. The Sergeant was the youngest man in the company; the sound of battle had brought back all his fire. To him numbers were nothing. He thought it now but a matter of a few hours, and France would be at the gates of Berlin. He saw once more the field of glory and heard again the shout of victory; Lorraine would be saved; he beheld the tricolor floating over the capital of the enemies of France. Perhaps, it would be planted there by Pierre. And he saw in his imagination Pierre climbing at a stride from a private to a captain, a colonel, a —! who could tell? — had not the *baton* been won in a campaign? As to dreaming that a battle could bring any other result than victory! — It was impossible!

"Where are you going?" shouted derisively the men of a regiment at rest, to the Sergeant's command as they marched past.

"To Berlin," replied the Sergeant.

The reply evoked cheers, and that regiment that day stood its ground until a fourth of its men fell. The old soldier's enthusiasm infected the new recruits, who were pale and nervous under the strain of waiting. His eye rested on Pierre, who was standing down near the other end of the company, and the father's face beamed as he thought he saw there resolution and impatience for the fight. Ha! France should ring with his name; the Quarter should go wild with delight.

Just then the skirmishers ahead began to fire, and in a few moments it was answered by a sullen note from the villages beyond the plain, and the battle had begun. The dropping fire of the skirmish line increased and merged into a rattle, and suddenly the thunder broke from a hill to their right, and ran along the crest until the earth trembled under their feet. Bullets began to whistle over their heads and clip the leaves of the trees beyond them, and the long, pulsating scream of shells flying over them and exploding in the park behind them made the faces of the men look gray in the morning twilight. Waiting was worse than fighting. It told on the young men.

In a little while a staff-officer galloped up to the colonel, who was sitting on his horse in the road, quietly smoking a cigar, and a moment later the whole line was in motion. They were wheeled to the right, and marched under shelter of the knoll in the direction of the firing. As they passed the turn of the road, they caught a glimpse of the hill ahead where the artillery, enveloped in smoke, was thundering from an ever-thickening cloud. A battery of eight guns galloped past them, and turning the curve disappeared in a cloud of dust. To the new recruits it seemed as if the whole battle was being fought right there. They could see nothing but their own line, and only a part of that; smoke and dust hid everything else; but the hill was plainly an important point, for they were being pushed forward, and the firing on the rise ahead of them was terrific. They were still partly protected by the ridge, but shells were screaming over them, and the earth was rocking under their feet. More batteries came thundering by, — the men clinging to the pieces and the drivers lashing their horses furiously, — and disappearing into the smoke on the hill, unlimbered and swelled the deafening roar; they passed men lying on the ground dead or wounded, or were passed by others helping wounded comrades to the rear. Several men in the company fell, some crying out or groaning with pain, and two or three killed outright.

The men were dodging and twisting, with heads bent forward a little as if in a pelting rain. Only the old Sergeant and some of the younger ones were perfectly erect.

" Why don't you dodge the balls? " asked a recruit of the Sergeant.

"A soldier of the empire never dodges," was the proud reply.

Some change occurred on the hills; they could not see what. Just then the order came down the line to advance at a double-quick and support the batteries. They moved forward at a run and passed beyond the shelter of the ridge. Instantly they were in the line of fire from the Prussian batteries, whose white puffs of smoke were visible across the plain, and bullets and shell tore wide spaces in their ranks. They could not see the infantrymen, who were in pits, but the bullets hissed and whistled by them. The men on both sides of Pierre were killed and fell forward on their faces with a thud, one of them still clutching his musket. Pierre would have stopped, but there was no time, the men in the rear pressed him on. As they appeared in the smoke of the nearest battery, the artillerymen broke into cheers at the welcome sight, and all down the line it was taken up. All around were dead and dying men increasing in numbers momentarily. No one had time to notice them. Some of them had blankets thrown over them. The infantry, who were a little to the side of the batteries, were ordered to lie down; most of them had already done so; even then they were barely protected; shot and shell ploughed the ground around them as if it had been a fallow field; men spoke to their comrades, and before receiving a reply were shot dead at their sides. The wounded were more ghastly than the dead; their faces growing suddenly deadly white from the shock as they were struck.

The gunners lay in piles around their guns, and still the survivors worked furiously in the dense heat and smoke, the sweat pouring down their blackened faces. The fire was terrific.

Suddenly an officer galloped up, and spoke to the lieutenant of the nearest battery.

" Where is the colonel ? "

" Killed."

" Where is your captain? "

" Dead, there under the gun."

"Are you in command ? "

" I suppose so."

" Well, hold this hill."

" How long ? "

" Forever." And he galloped off.

His voice was heard clear and ringing in a sudden lull, and the old Sergeant, clutching his musket, shouted:

"We will, forever."

There was a momentary lull.

Suddenly the cry was:

" Here they are."

In an instant a dark line of men appeared coming up the slope. The guns were trained down on them, but shot over their heads; they were double shotted and trained lower, and belched forth canister. They fell in swathes, yet still they came on at a run, hurrahing, until they were almost up among the guns, and the gunners were leaving their pieces. The old Sergeant's voice speaking to his men was as steady as if on parade, and kept them down, and when the command was given to fire kneeling, they rose as one man, and poured a volley into the Germans' faces which sent them reeling back down the hill, leaving a broken line of dead and struggling men on the deadly crest. Just then a brigade officer came along. They heard him say, " That repulse may stop them." Then he gave some order in an undertone to the lieutenant in command of the batteries, and passed on. A moment later the fire from the Prussian batteries was heavier than before; the guns were being knocked to pieces. A piece of shell struck the Sergeant on the cheek, tearing away the flesh badly. He tore the sleeve from his shirt and tied it around his head with perfect unconcern. The fire of the Germans was still growing heavier; the smoke was too dense to see a great deal,

but they were concentrating or were coming
closer. The lieutenant came back for a moment and spoke to the captain of the company, who, looking along the line, called the
Sergeant, and ordered him to go back down
the hill to where the road turned behind it,
and tell General —— to send them a support
instantly, as the batteries were knocked to
pieces, and they could not hold the hill much
longer. The announcement was astonishing
to the old soldier; it had never occurred
to him that as long as a man remained they
could not hold the hill, and he was half-way
down the slope before he took it in. He had
brought his gun with him, and he clutched
it convulsively as if he could withstand alone
the whole Prussian army. "He might have
taken a younger man to do his trotting," he
muttered to himself as he stalked along, not
knowing that his wound had occasioned his
selection. "Pierre —" but, no, Pierre must
stay where he would have the opportunity to
distinguish himself.

It was no holiday promenade that the old
soldier was taking; for his path lay right
across the track swept by the German batteries, and the whole distance was strewn

with dead, killed as they had advanced in the morning. But the old Sergeant got safely across. He found the General with one or two members of his staff sitting on horseback in the road near the park gate, receiving and answering dispatches. He delivered his message.

"Go back and tell him he *must* hold it," was the reply. "Upon it depends the fate of the day; perhaps of France. Or wait, you are wounded; I will send some one else; you go to the rear." And he gave the order to one of his staff, who saluted and dashed off on his horse. "Hold it for France," he called after him.

The words were heard perfectly clear even above the din of battle which was steadily increasing all along the line, and they stirred the old soldier like a trumpet. No rear for him! He turned and pushed back up the hill at a run. The road had somewhat changed since he left, but he marked it not; shot and shell were ploughing across his path more thickly, but he did not heed them; in his ears rang the words — "For France." They came like an echo from the past; it was the same cry he had heard at Waterloo, when the soldiers of France that summer day had died for France and the emperor, with a cheer on their lips. "For France": the words were consecrated; the emperor himself had used them. He had heard him, and would have died then; should he not die now for her! Was it not glorious to die for France, and have men say that he had fought for her when a babe, and had died for her when an old man!

With these thoughts was mingled the thought of Pierre — Pierre also would die for France! They would save her or die together; and he pressed his hand with a proud caress over the cross on his breast. It was the emblem of glory.

He was almost back with his men now; he knew it by the roar, but the smoke hid everything. Just then it shifted a little. As it did so, he saw a man steal out of the dim line and start towards him at a run. He had on the uniform of his regiment. His cap was pulled over his eyes, and he saw him deliberately fling away his gun. He was skulking. All the blood boiled up in the old soldier's veins. Desert! — not fight for France! Why did not Pierre shoot him! Just then the coward passed close to him, and the old man seized him with a grip of iron. The deserter, surprised, turned his face; it was pallid with terror and shame; but no more so than his captor's. It was Pierre.

"Pierre!" he gasped. "Good God! where are you going?"

"I am sick," faltered the other.

"Come back," said the father sternly.

"I cannot," was the terrified answer.

"It is for France, Pierre," pleaded the old soldier.

"Oh! I cannot," moaned the young man, pulling away. There was a pause — the old man still holding on hesitatingly, then, — "Dastard!" he hissed, flinging his son from him with indescribable scorn.

Pierre, free once more, was slinking off with averted face, when a new idea seized his father, and his face grew grim as stone. Cocking his musket, he flung it up, took careful and deliberate aim at his son's retreating figure, and brought his finger slowly down upon the trigger. But, before he could fire, a shell exploded directly in the line of his aim, and when the smoke blew off, Pierre had disappeared. The Sergeant lowered his piece, gazed curiously down the hill, and then hurried to the spot where the shell had burst. A mangled form marked the place. The coward had in the very act of flight met the death he dreaded. Pierre lay dead on his face, shot in the back. The back of his head was shattered by a fragment of shell. The countenance of the living man was more pallid than that of the dead. No word escaped him, except that refrain, "For France, for France," which he repeated mechanically.

Although this had occupied but a few minutes, momentous changes had taken place on the ridge above. The sound of the battle had somewhat altered, and with the roar of artillery were mingled now the continuous rattle of the musketry and the shouts and cheers of the contending troops. The fierce onslaught of the Prussians had broken the line somewhere beyond the batteries, and the French were being borne back. Almost immediately the slope was filled with retreating men hurrying back in the demoralization of panic. All order was lost. It was a rout. The soldiers of his own regiment began to rush by the spot where the old Sergeant stood above his son's body. Recognizing him, some of his comrades seized his arm and attempted to hurry him along; but with a fierce exclamation the old soldier shook them off, and raising his voice so that he was heard even above the tumult of the rout, he shouted, "Are ye all cowards? Rally for France — For France ——"

They tried to bear him along; the officers, they said, were dead; the Prussians had captured the guns, and had broken the whole line. But it was no use; still he shouted that rallying cry, For France, for France, "Vive la France; Vive l'Empereur"; and steadied by the war-cry, and accustomed to obey an officer, the men around him fell instinctively into something like order, and for an instant the rout was arrested. The fight was renewed over Pierre's dead body. As they had, however, truly said, the Prussians were too strong for them. They had carried the line and were now pouring down the hill by thousands in the ardor of hot pursuit, the line on either side of the hill was swept away, and whilst the gallant little band about the old soldier still stood and fought desperately, they were soon surrounded. There was no thought of quarter; none was asked, none was given. Cries, curses, cheers, shots, blows, were mingled together, and clear above all rang the old soldier's war-cry, For France, for France, " Vive la France, Vive l'Empereur." It was the refrain from an older and bloodier field. He thought he was at Waterloo.

Mad with excitement, the men took up the cry, and fought like tigers ; but the issue could not be doubtful.

Man after man fell, shot or clubbed down, with the cry " For France " on his lips, and his comrades, standing astride his body, fought with bayonets and clubbed muskets till they too fell in turn. Almost the last one was the old Sergeant. Wounded to death, and bleeding from numberless gashes, he still fought, shouting his battle-cry, " For France," till his musket was hurled spinning from his shattered hand, and staggering sense-less back, a dozen bayonets were driven into his breast, crushing out forever the brave spirit of the soldier of the empire.

It was best, for France was lost.

A few hours later the Quarter was in mourning over the terrible defeat.

*　　*　　*　　*　　*

That night a group of Prussian officers go-ing over the field with lanterns looking after their wounded, stopped near a spot remarkable even on that bloody slope for the heaps of dead of both armies literally piled upon each other.

"It was just here," said one, "that they got reinforcements and made that splendid rally."

A second, looking at the body of an old French sergeant lying amidst heaps of slain, with his face to the sky, said simply as he saw his scars:

"There died a brave soldier."

Another, older than the first, bending closer to count the bayonet wounds, caught the gleam of something in the light of the lantern, and stooping to examine a broken cross of the Legion on the dead man's breast, said reverently:

"He was a *soldier of the empire.*"

Typography by J. S. Cushing & Co., Boston.

Presswork by Berwick & Smith, Boston.